SANTO

SANTO

A NOVEL

Jared Walsh

SCAFFOLDS PRESS

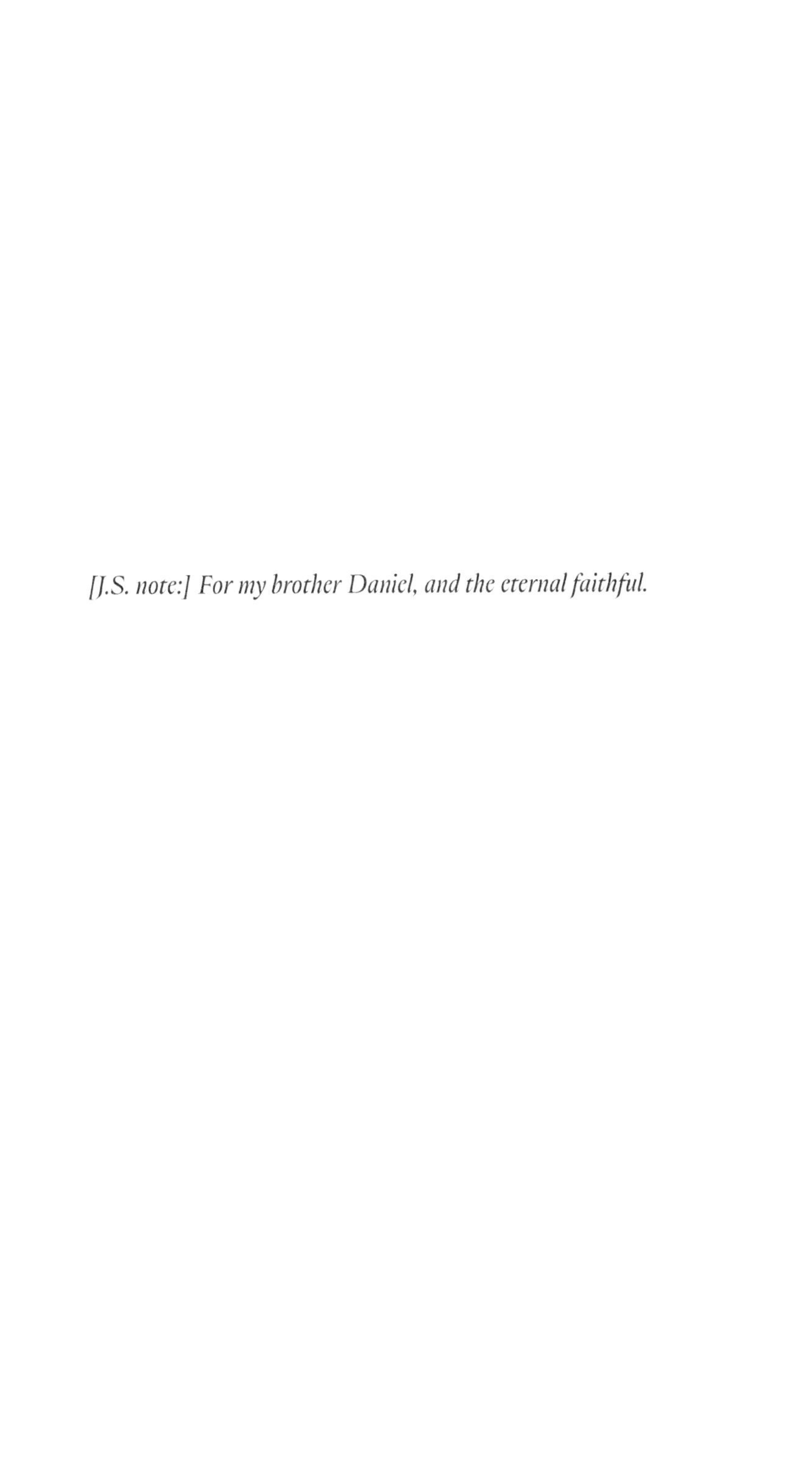

[J.S. note:] For my brother Daniel, and the eternal faithful.

PART ONE

1

A Nobel Prize. Two kids, a wife, a tenured professorship, many other—unspeakables. I cannot decide who belongs where, I cannot decide what is what. I cannot decide if I am man or beast, soul or shell, blessed or damned.

That is just the surface of life, that is just the part I can describe in plain language. I could refer you to any number of suicides, real or fictional, bodily or spiritual, announced or latent, whose story tracks mine. Fame— disillusionment—exitus. I however am taking a wrong turn on the way to my denouement. At the moment of the highest inertia, in the first scene of the final act, when men, despondent, begin to count down their slow descent to the grave, I am headed back to the origins of my existence.

Before I got on this plane, I observed the beings, the remnants of humanity in the airport. They lingered, heads down, eyes down, surrendered to the blind blade of the guillotine. Who will rescue them?

Who will lift their eyes to the horizon once more? And will it matter?

This kind of talk is all as old as the world, as old as the holy ghost. I do not have to educate you as to the duality of fate. It is all what I am running from. Flying in fact, not running. I am gone.

<h1 style="text-align:center">2</h1>

When you leave what I left, it almost doesn't matter where you are going. How many nights spent screaming in the bathroom without a sound. Ablutions do force out the emotions. How many nights would I have given my life for a ticket straight to Hell.

Blood to flow. Give me my own blood to flow, just for me to witness it. As proof of life. I almost said this to Sofia—but she wouldn't understand. She would hit me with something upside the head and dislodge my mind, and the blood would crust over and heal, and mean nothing. I packed up, breathed a final kiss into her forehead, breathed kisses into the portraits of my children, now grown and gone . . .

Then release, doubt, bravery in the taxi, euphoria in the airport. A smoke shop was open. I bought a hundred thousand Dunhills. Down where I am going, there is not a proper cigarette, they cut them with sugar. Nor is there a proper shower, or a proper newspaper nor blunderbuss flattery nor men and women acting like the horrors of horrors. Nor sense of time. Just me and the one woman who is not a woman. She is the Earth. And you can only get into her through the middle—the wet part between two oceans.

These are not Miller's Tropics. Miller did, eventually, find something out about what happens to a man when he escapes the tyranny of his birth country. He fled to Paris, he fled to Greece. He was a lover of mankind. And I share his hatred for materialism. But I do not share his special feel for the current of an age, of a society, of a people. I am too much of an individualist to imagine that my thoughts and feelings can be generalized past myself. So, I will not make this journal into anything referential or symbolic. It is my account of the last part of my life, and nothing more.

I will try to be rougher, more textured than the voice that pronounces the truth. I no longer believe in truth. But I do believe in the dismemberment of dissimulation. It takes hard work. We are so layered with lies. Most of those lies are "truths."

We are flying over Cuba. The lights are chaotic, starform, starstruck. I thought I was looking down at the sky after the rigid order of Florida, which looks at night like a Communist nightmare. I already cannot imagine ever going back home. Florida . . . Cuba . . . then black. The black gives me the greatest comfort.

3

___

We descended from the plane. The air was full of heat and moisture and scents of rotting leaves and fires. The volcanoes watched over us, they loomed dark and misted and alive over the domain as they always have, but even larger and even more powerful than I remember them—especially Rincón de la Vieja. The hills of California, the Alps of Switzerland are beautiful. The Caribbean slope of Rincón, the summit ridge of Cacao are different, when you know what is up there. Not a numen or a monster, not the ghost of your dead forbears. Not god, not gods, not Nature, not this, not that. I consider it the job of the rest of my life to describe what is up there, and I do not expect it to be easy.

Just as the volcanoes have veiled themselves in mystery, I have made myself known in Costa Rica to a very few individuals—blood brothers and blood sisters, fellow explorers of the unknown, who are in many ways closer to me than my own family. Outside this circle, no one hears my voice or witnesses my movements unless that voice is giving a lecture on *Lepidoptera* and those movements are gesticulations meant to demonstrate academic discipline and obsession. I cannot have it broadcast about that the Swedish Academy made a fatal error. I will write more on this later, or never. Do I have an audience? Does it matter?

One of these blood brothers, Ilario, picked me up from the airport. He drove my most prized possession—the Toyota HJ45 I bought in La Cruz in 1989. We drove together in relative quiet through the late afternoon chatter and street dust of Liberia and up the Interamerican towards Santa Rosa. I smoked my first two cigarettes of the season. He declined and declined, and finally had one. We opened a couple of beers. They felt the way they are supposed to feel—like a transfiguration of the mind. I will drink many beers this time I am here—many more beers than I have drunk in the past. My mind needs to be destroyed and built up again brick by brick.

I am sitting on my bed with my snake, a giant boa constrictor named Smiley, in a shack the CIA once used to house the men who helped arm the Contras against the Sandinistas. The shack was, and is, very well proportioned. There is a front porch for the main room and there are side porches for the bedrooms. In order to access certain of the bedrooms, you have to walk outside, which gives the inhabitants a sense of false privacy (for ventilation, the walls do not reach the ceilings). The kitchen and the shower are lit through an abundance of glass blocks. The common room is large enough to house a meeting of a good number of killers at a generous round table. Along the longest wall, at about eye height, there is a concrete ledge that must have been contemplated as a library shelf. Many of the old CIA folks were Yalies. There is no hot water, but you don't miss it, because the air itself is hot enough to turn a cold shower into deliverance. The toilet is in its own little water closet, in a European flourish used not uncommonly in this country.

I am sitting on my bed with Smiley, who graciously made his way to the porch once he caught word that I was coming. There are doves hooting all over the drive-way, around which cluster three other shack-villas like mine. The light of the day is coming down, and I am about to do something I have done since my twenti-eth year, when I first arrived in Santa Rosa. I am going to put on Carl Orff and get monstrously drunk, very slowly. In fact I have already started the process. It involves a good rum called Centenario.

All bodies are now as black as night, they have lost their color. The trees, the birds black as night. The dis-tance, the closeness. I cannot hear the sea but I can feel its air—and in that air an oceanic restlessness. My women fly away one by one. My cares, my curae—to go aloft as the birds, to circle back.

It matters where we are, because the mind fills the space it is given. At home, my mind filled the bereft landscape of my townhome in Cambridge, and it filled the orbits of my younger son, who is troubled. And it filled sometimes the dishwasher and the sink. And it filled the lifeless whiteness of the pages of scientific journals. And it filled the narrow gauge of my wife's thoughts—her stockings and her lipstick collections and her bowel movements. It filled the closeness of the lecture hall, where my words would fall on scraping, unquestioning ears. It filled the absurdity of a Mercedes, where old men go to perish gracefully with their carcasses caressed by the cabin heater. It filled the dead spaces of the bars, where I cringed even to take a drink in the glare of the televisions. Now all of that is gone, flown, gone, flown, to fly back again in triple nightmares and dead shakes and drab panics.

Orff is approaching his third revolution. I let him go on repeat. He is singing about the vicissitudes of fate.

4

It is still dark, though the birds are starting to awaken. I have already lost my moorings.

The sweet smell of leaf rot flies on the wind. Rot alive, not yet ripe, never to fall nor to be consumed. An accident, because there is no intention out here, there is chaos, there is something beyond chaos. The curtain of night ripples a faint portent of the dawn. Here she comes.

What are you—Santa Rosa? She is in me, I am in her. She is out there, she is everywhere. I may never find her.

Years ago—many years ago—thirty years ago or more—you skinned your coccyx on the rough stone of the monument. The cut was infected. You took impure water and you were doubly ill. Yet you stayed with me until you could not take the intensity anymore.

Bats scratched the sky. Volcanoes lay quiet under lightning. Don't leave me yet, I said, in that shot dark. The same dark as this one. The same night as this night. The same landscape. The same silence.

You were the last one who was able to put her arms around the entire James Santo. What to do with such a prize, so early on in life? It was just before I married Sofia.

You used to say, nature does not know names, hours, cities, bodies. I just threw my watch into the woods. It is late, early, dark, dawning. I threw my watch into the woods and said a small prayer to the Milky Way, which shines above me bright as a belt of fire. Protect my family, and protect you, bless you—bless you more than anyone. I may not ever be back.

Don't leave me yet, I said. You remained silent. I reflect now, with the first wave of the calls of the wrens and rails, that independence is gained solely through abandonment—and through that blood-bespattered lens I owe you the rest of my life.

They call this dry forest. Half the year everything starves. Half the year everything feasts. Tens of thousands of species—the names of which do not begin to tell of their origins, of their innate artistry—starve and feast as they may.

Every year there is a dark age, a plague, a Renaissance.

And the best part—these creatures want from us nothing at all. Leading us to want from them: visits, and eternity.

Hummingbirds visit my *Heliconia* every morning

and afternoon. They too shun the brightest and the darkest times. The stasis of the sun, the permanence of the dark. When there is no hope of deliverance, and we have forgotten from what, and to what.

5

It is the third day now. Last night the storms rolled in heavy and hypnotizing in their psychotic fury. We had a gathering of sorts. Two young Italian primatologists cooked porcinis on the porch. Park staff made an appearance. My assistants emerged from a Land Cruiser baptized in mud. I looked at them. I looked away. I looked at them. I looked away.

I hired Alicia and Felicia solely on the power of their resumes—I assumed that their outstanding marks in Ecology, Systematics, Organic Chemistry, Physics, Linear Algebra, Statistics, and Continental Philosophy would promise me two quietly diligent, ideally outright homely, and at the very least awkward and asexual assistants. Detached, depressed and aloof as I was this past semester, I never thought to waste time interviewing my seasonal labor. Another foolish, fatal error in James Santo's judgement.

I looked at them. I looked away. They looked at me. They looked away.

6

—

Day four. I laid out an experiment on paper. Now that I've done all I am capable of on the world stage, I am back to the investigation of the very minuscule. I will spend this summer tracking the tendencies of the army ants and asking after their origins. This is a question that has bothered us here for years. What is their impetus to mass murder and mass suicide? If I am to pose even an approach at an answer, I should be fully absorbed in this question. But I am absorbed by another question, one that resides deeper inside me than any objective inquiry can reach.

During the first few weeks in the Tropics, the entire being goes through a painful process of self-cleansing, and for me the cleansing takes the shape of a band of nightmares. People in my dreams keep coming by and asking me: Why? And offering their advice—two things that always disgusted me most. And I am made to bear coffins for those whose coffins I bore as a young man—my grandparents, my uncles, my brother Daniel.

I am made to wait in hotel rooms for mistresses who never come or who come but do not know me, or do not want anything. Made to wait for the ones I made wait for me. A treatment I richly deserve.

But I have also made myself wait. What of that? Whom to punish?

The light outside is so heavy that it drills you into the ground, and so is the air—heavy with rain and mist. I go outside and I want to swat it. I smoke so that the air next to me feels comparatively refreshing.

I walked today with my two assistants. We walked over ten kilometers, to identify the bivouacs we would begin to study. The army ants build palaces out of live bodies, a feat that was not lost on me when, decades ago, I awoke to suspect that I had slept in some Chinese garden under a black gaslight in which untold vapors roiled. They roiled some more. And from that gaslight hundreds of pincers and pins and needles descended on me. I was lucky to have a face, said the doctor, chuckling, until a stray ant crawled up his arm and nabbed him in the soft flesh just south of the armpit. He screamed like a child.

The ants move in consistent confusion, each knowing the other but not knowing each. It is a lucky mind that does not know its own mind, but knows enough of the minds of others to go about its business. The rest is flesh that knows only flesh.

For some reason the slave instinct of the ants reminds me of my father.

"One day, it is possible, I think, that I might save a million dollars," he used to say.

He did not save a million dollars, and though he had accomplished far greater feats as a researcher and an educator and a public servant, this basic worldly failure nagged him until the end of his days. He fell down the basement staircase with the intention of reading the label on an empty paint can. So said my mother, who saw it happen, and collected a million dollars of life insurance. She burned half a million cigarettes before she quit, smoking and living, cold turkey over her cereal.

Fine, I thought. Fine. I re-arranged her hands, which had curdled together as the milk she had poured over her corn flakes. And I re-arranged the glasses that had fallen crooked across her face when she hit the table.

I got drunk with Allan Mayfield last night. He curates the *Lepidoptera* collection at the British Museum. In his youth he could outdrink and outfuck anything. Now he is retired from all that, or better said Emeritus. He is still in great shape from having hunted butterflies in the field his entire life. He told me that in twenty years the incomparably elegant, playful, and elusive *Adelpha leucophthalma tegeata* would be extinct. I told him she will go where her *Pentagonia* thrives, and that may be further windward on the Caribbean slopes of the cordillera, but she will not disappear. We smoked fistfuls of my Dunhills. We got drunk to the point where I believed I was sober again. The conversation turned to the subject Allan and I revisit the most. He asked me to perorate on you. He remembers you—all too well.

You were not quite real to me, in the flesh. You are far more real to me now.

Why hide one face under another one? Speak in scientific terms, but not of scientific things. This is going to be a difficult exercise. The unburning of a forest fire.

From what to what?

Child to man—man to Child.

All of my women strike in silhouette the same figure. The same dark spot on my mind's eye. And the same blinding bright spot in some other light. I am unable to keep them from bleeding into one another. Over all that ambiguity, you drape yourself like the cosmos.

7

I am dark guinea. Epiphytes grow out of my ears. Abstract crowns of palm trees sprout out of my nostrils. My stomach is taut like the stomach of a young child. My muscles are holdovers from another century. The crop on my head is thinning, while the one on my face is thickening. My reflection is windblown, and tired.

There is an advantage to seeming so broken down. I am past the point of vanity, so my mind often feels like it has unoccupied space—the space that would otherwise house my machinery of self-absorption. I no longer rethink a statement after it has escaped my mouth, for example, even if I know the statement was hyperbolic or invented, and even if I should be ashamed of ever having said it. I often reflect upon how many days I spent, in my life, scheming a defense of my pride instead of inhabiting the realm of ideas. I did not even know the difference between the two. Hence I authored as many articles as the journals would print. Some were very close replicas of one another. Some were meditations on imaginary answers to imaginary questions. Many upon many were statistical fabrications. With one goal—to aggrandize the status and indirectly the bank account of the author. Now Sofia pours all that out on my Afghan rugs.

Not until I realized that my body was conclusively worn did I look away from the mirror and start to consider what I would contribute to the world before I left it. By that point my mind had also been warped by time and intoxication, such that the old theories I had lived by no longer made sense. This was the period when I reordered the universe in my head and sold that alternate vision to the public, to governments, to corporations, to princes and to peasants. Something could be saved, something could be salvaged of this incomparable natural world if we only worked up the restraint to leave it alone . . . .

Now the empty space in my head is just empty, it is peaceful, it is peace itself. I can go into that Japanese tea room and sit there, Indian style, in my mind, anytime I want. I have no need of change. I have no need of progress. And most of all I have no need of validation.

Disadvantage of no women—no food. Today I invited my assistants to move from the main dormitory to my quarters. They were happy to be rid of the bickering Italian primatologists and shack up with ye olde savage.

I woke up this morning in the perfect place—the sunlight, alone. The girls had gone to the ocean. The ocean—Playa Nancite especially—washes away our sins. It is a pilgrimage that must be made on foot in the wet season, and I am not ready yet.

Adaptation is pure chance out here. I cannot want it, I cannot seek it consciously. It comes to me unnamed and unawares, just like that. Whoosh! And I am part of the landscape. I can stand in the sun for hours without burning, I can stand in the rain for hours without getting wet. I leave the house in the morning without eating but without being hungry, and I walk for miles, just looking. I start recognizing certain individual trees again, trees who have through the centuries reached unwaveringly for the blue nothing in nameless places without a witness, trees whose hearts are as pure as the wind, and I embrace them as I would my brothers.

When my thoughts stop making sense, I am beginning, but just beginning, to acclimatize. Pieces of shade can crack and freeze. The basilisk. The obelisk. Distant, very distant memories of poplars. A park rolling down to the sea.

When my thoughts reach a level of mildness so that they almost disappear.

The girls clean the house, usually when they are stoned. Then, after dark, the forest velvet, we search out visions on the inner surfaces of our eyelids. Remembered faces, for me, materialize in sandstone perfection. My mind unravels—with my wife as the background—and I abandon her to gain the thread. Then I search for her like a dog dragging his leash about town. How typical of man to yearn for that which has beaten him within an inch of his life.

I have a bandana with which I ring my bald head. This is the same one I wore when my hair was so long and dense it flew behind me like a black flame. The same one I wore back when I had no fear of time ever passing.

$$8$$

Last night I had a dream of a man who wanted to kill us, but could not make up his mind on how—

God—

He had a long dark face, Italian, like the Pope—an old Pope, Alexander or Julius. Always immaculately dressed and moving too quickly for me to achieve his attention.

At one point he drowned us in a cave.

Alicia, Felicia floated by. I could not cry—

My last breath was held. The cave dried up, and the sunlight penetrated. Other trials ensued.

There was a charity gala that turned to chaos. There was a chase through a library to the roof of a skyscraper, from which I cannot remember if I jumped.

All this rich dreaming was the fault of the sounds outside that declared over me their supremacy. The rain has been pounding these metal roofs. There is darkness that no invention of man can penetrate. Darkness has a sound—the creatures wail the same message to one another—they wail for us to give in so that they can turn us under, grain by grain, back to soil. Lock by lock to reeds. Flaw by flaw to riverbeds. Tear by tear to seas. And so on. The idea of God—as a wily magician with some curiosity invested in everyone's life—derives from all this. Up there on the roof of the skyscraper—before I jumped or did not jump—he took my mind and pulled it out of my skull and floated it next to me, just so. He made me look at it and asked me, do you see fear there? Do you see knowledge there? Or do you see something else? Madness? And what is the symbol of madness? It is an ocean that wanders forever and is not lost but not quite located in any one place.

The girls want to go to Nancite again. They want a sense of forgiveness that this dense, darkly enchanted landscape cannot always give. I tell them let us go to the chaparral, the pampas, the open hills of Santa Elena. But they are set on another pilgrimage. So, I told them, take your pilgrimage. I would never have loosed my staff so easily in the old days, but I am becoming increasingly convinced that the organisms will do what they do whether we watch them or not.

9

My assistants have similar names. Alicia—Felicia—the two sides of happiness. Not bought, but created. Not created, but incarnate. Academics have a way of saying, "not this, but that", and making it sound like they are saying something. Bismarck was not vile, but simply too often drunk. The weeds in the wild are not weeds, but wonders. Evolution is not evolution, but a sideways dance inside a hall of mirrors. I spent my life studying natural history, but it matters not what came before, in the physicality of the present.

Alicia—Felicia—they believe that I am a man of genius. I am trying to show them that genius, under the surface, is nothing but stubborn, unwavering diligence. And the willingness to fail spectacularly.

They want to know the names of things. Not to know them, but to also to hear me say them. My voice to me sounds broken down, but I do say them.

Rothschildia lebeau

Cotinis mutabilis

Dysdercus lunulatus

Latin is the most seductive language, because it is unspoken and feels forbidden and smells of churches.

Pulchra = beautiful

A woman in her pulchritude. Ten days of nightmares and already I fiend for deliverance. It is a delightful feeling, actually, this hunger, and I am not sure I want it sated at all.

I need a walk. I have not yet taken a true walk. I have stayed in our shotgun shack and listened to the rain and slept while the sun was out and sought demons when it was not and have generally stayed stoned and drunk—it helps me forget about my family.

10

—

I took the truck out into the mountains of Santa Elena. I am exposed. Interplanetary winds scroll my face and give texture to the sunlight. Everything in motion that only a violin can capture. Blind, capricious, devastating. Nature is the sworn enemy of mathematics. And I, for a generation, have thrown statistics at it. Now I give up. There is no way.

From here I can see the sea. Its mouth is open wide like a wild blue fire. What does it want? Whose sacrifice?

It is impossible to remember thoughts. Thank god I have chosen to write them down, this once. I lost so many things with my hands in the waterfall, thinking I was catching them. Just as I lived my life for the feeling of friction as I passed through people.

The air is thickening with vapor and light. Five minutes outside my truck, and I expire from walking. There are lives behind this one—that much becomes clear.

I can phrase the conceit differently—without regard to time. There are so many lives in my midst, from sun, to sky, to orchid, to live oak, to blade of grass—to viper—so many lives that life itself seems not to matter. Then what?

I do not wish anything . . .

. . . now suddenly I do.

Do I want to admit even to myself what that wish is? It has nothing to do with bugs, or birds, or ferns, or trees, or fame. Those are just endless mysteries to distract me from wishes that can only be human.

My sons—will they know this? Will they know my defeat? I fear they know it already. So many doors. They say you can only pick one. I have picked them all. When I am done, I will wake up for a moment, and the dream will begin again.

The clouds are transcribing a message in the blue. Painting something, and with greater furor and with greater clarity than any master. A girl's face takes shape from her chin, frowns, makes an arrowhead, which is translated into a whole landscape of island, sea, sky. How? Who? Out here in the world, there is perfect order and perfect discord. Are there any other choices? Is there anything in between?

You cannot ever prove that a cause or a thing is utterly beyond your knowledge, because in order to say that, you need to know where that cause or thing exists. So, if I said, the landscape that spreads out before me is the entire world in a nutshell, there would be no way to disprove that statement. So let me adopt that statement, for the sake of adopting something:

This expanse of Santa Elena is the entire world—the planet, the universe—in its inviolate state—before all was lost. (See my open hands.)

Alicia and Felicia left their beds this morning, before I awoke. I have a feeling, every minute or so, as to where their tiny feet might be falling on those wisp-like forest paths that I blazed over the decades.

I cannot say that my ideas, my feelings, are not in fact knowledge. And I cannot say that they are. It is this way with everything. Everything, for us, is in the third space, between prophecy and pandemonium.

11

—

I killed one of the road doves on the way back here tonight. At the bar there was a mechanical bull. Is that prophecy?

Very drunk.

God or nature or that third thing maybe. Maybe this is not the right question. Maybe. Simply. God is the wrong word. Nature is the wrong word.

What

Am I doing?

I am trying to come clean to myself. Not even to myself, it seems, have I ever spoken a word of truth. The original sin is that all these years, I have claimed that a truth exists, and claimed to speak it. From that point on, and including that point, I lied.

How many sloths, out of all sloths living, will give you an evil smile?

It is not possible to care about a number. I do not care about a number. What I do care about is the one. I care about the one. The identity of the one is uncertain, and her attributes change whether I view her in gold, in blue shade, in the red light in between, in stasis, in motion or in flight. Her attributes change depending on how I see myself. At times her identity forks, and forks again. It is you, and it is not you.

Now, you see, language has less and less to say about this dilemma. Only life can speak to art, and only art can speak to life. As the paint is absorbed by the canvas, it is at once gained and lost.

12

You say that the human is higher than the monkey. But the monkey is higher than the human—he is up in the trees, we are down on the ground. He is up with the dawn, down with the dusk, as the sun intends. From monkey to human is as falcon to salmon. Out of the sky, we are back in the water. We swim upriver all our lives, and at the source, we die of desire and go dry. There is your evolution.

Even this fanciful family tree attempts to draw a line in space where there is no line. The concept of genus, the concept of species—are naught but a form of fantasy that allows a person to nod and move on—where he perhaps ought to be pausing, and wondering—the two fig trees outside my window—are they the same? In what ways are they not? My eyes have roughly the same shape as Theodore Roosevelt's. You could say that we are one. I am, he was, the same type of thing.

And so?

The identification of a person's species says as little about him as the identification of what planet he is on. Why do we imagine we are saying something, when we identify the species of a different sort of thing? Trees do not understand English—or Latin.

Alicia—she comes to me with diagrams. She has it in her fine little brain that ants have been classified all cockeyed. That we should look past their color—some reddish, some blackish—indeed beyond their physical appearance entirely—to their very families. Since the concept of species has less to do with color and shape than with the question of who is fucking whom. In the case of a polyamorous queen, the situation gets complicated. Alicia has identified thirty-three families of *Eciton burchellii* within a ten minute walk of our shotgun shack. Her impetus, I gather, is that she is good at naming names.

Anastasia . . . Coronado . . . Baleara . . . Dipsomatia . . . go the families.

Felicia—she is more interested in the scouts, the wanderers, the lost ones. She follows lone ants into the unmapped wilderness. She comes back late, and other times comes back not at all. She will sleep in the cradle of a fig tree's roots with the venomous snakes in her midst, her body famished and deflated under her clothes, and her mind on the threshold of illegible madness. In her sleep even, she will reach for what cannot be expressed. She wants to be a witness to something happening one time, in the utter loneliness of the forest, and never again.

Probably when Felicia was small, when she smoked for the visual effect—now she does it for the slight rush of suffocation—and waited at night to be stolen away—when she had reasons for things, this urge to be intentionally lost struck her as just one among her many affectations.

But I speak to myself in the language of humanity, which is obsessed with origins . . . .

Maybe there was no origin to Felicia's special breed of psyche. There certainly do not seem to be any origins to mine. None that I can trace, and what would tracing mean? Eh James?

Alicia gets fully formed ideas delivered to her with breakfast, she has the infinite faces of the prism built up in her mind's eye as a theorem. Felicia does not allow her mind to form any preconceived theories of the world. Hence one returns with diagrams and tiny notes and new names for things that have already been identified, and the other returns with bruises.

Of whom am I enamored more? Curse the night that brought me to that question. I have traveled millions of years back in time—to arrive at the same question I was trying to leave back home. But perhaps the idea that I am even capable of ennobling myself in any climate, in any epoch, is merely a delusion of the cities, the papers, the universities, the censors. There is no nobility in nature.

In the end all questions will all untie themselves and reveal that inside, they are all wind, sky, the sounds of the night, the great plateau of Santa Rosa, the moonscape of Santa Elena. Or can I actually say that they have already done so—and that I am busy feathering through fossils. There is the possibility that we are in fact spending our lives this way—feathering through artefacts of our expired philosophies—like a chimpanzee playing with his own shit.

If I listen hard enough to the wilds, even the concept of death feels merely like a relic. Because in geologic time, it will happen so soon that it is essentially over. Out here, I am not so much afraid of death as I am afraid of life.

13

The skies threatened rain all morning, yet the rain passed over us for Orosi, Cacao, and Rincón, over which it looms as a black mist. The girls too went through the day with their heads in the clouds. They seemed to upbraid anything that asked them to exist. So I did not. I told them to visit the bivouacs and just observe, do not write anything down, do not form any opinions.

In this heavy air the frogs are having a continuous orgy.

I went to town. The people of La Cruz are sitting on sidewalks, on tractors and on hoods. Strange exposure, the town to nature. So dirty, yet not dirty enough. The whole should be made of mud, or just painted brown. Instead, it blinds me with whitewash. The wide embrace of Bahia Salinas ripples below.

I went to the gas station. I filled the Cruiser with diesel. When I first bought her she had no clutch, so I had to match the ratios to shift gears. I had to start her in first gear and she would lurch forward and into per-petual motion. At stoplights it was a risky little calcu-lation of how long I could drift. I was patient with her. I, too, was born without any kind of neutral.

Something changed on Felicia's face tonight. We had started a conversation on our observation of the behaviors of lowland versus highland *Nymphalids*, but it had spiraled many times, many loops out of control from there. And her face, which rests day to day in a kind of intellectual smirk, changed over to a lost com-plexity I have not seen for a very long time. It gave me a shiver I am still fighting, somewhere deep down in the roots of the spine.

The conversation turned to politics, and I let it stay there. Agony over what we cannot change is all part of the purging that must happen down here. The agony happens, and that is the only way for it to flow out of us.

Carter, Reagan, the Ayatollah, the Queen. Marx, Fidel, and all the suckers and saints. Khrushchev, Kennedy, Mussolini, Hitler. Lindbergh. Sinatra. The Rough Riders. Hell's Angels. The Grateful Dead. Steinbeck, Pound, Proust, Lord Byron. Agamemnon, Achilles, Paris, Lesbos, and the Swineherd. Hannibal, Scipio, Augustus, Caligula, Trajan, Marco Polo, Chinggis Khan, Timur the Lame, Ain Jalut, and Jesus Christ. Pope Julius. Henry the Fourth. Henry the Fifth. Bottom, Titania, Falstaff, and Pope. Harriet Tubman, the Tiger, Harper's Ferry,

Franklin, Grant, Lincoln, Kennedy, Carter, and Reagan.

So reality's snake coils round our minds, it tightens its grip, then mysteriously lets us go. Felicia—the little devil. And Alicia—her obverse. I just want to sit still and mute with her until she stops crying and goes to sleep.

I got us all very high tonight. On my way home from La Cruz I visited my friend, a retired lawyer who lives in a shack by Cuajiniquil. For as long as I have been coming down here, this particular friend has been a retired lawyer sitting in a shack by Cuajiniquil. He retired at thirty-five, when his wife left him for a German hotelier. He has a library and a roof and a mosquito net and a Range Rover. He has a makeshift jakes and a makeshift shower, consisting of a hose connected to a bucket connected to a chain. And without fail, he has a pile of marijuana about as large as you can make one without endangering the angle of repose. He has made his life philosophizing and shooting pool. After so many years, he does not sell me drugs. He reaches into his pile, grabs a number of generous handfuls, and ties them up in a plastic bag as a care package. His weed is a beautiful mild smoke that the three of us can sip on all evening with our beers. Then about fifteen minutes later it takes your mind and squeezes it through an oculus at the top of your skull and floats it in the air like a soap bubble.

I can still hear laughter from the girls' room. Fairly soon I am going to have to tie myself to a tree or deport myself to avoid the inevitable.

14

Alicia came back this evening past sundown, wet from weeping and faint. One of her colonies had lost its queen. She arrived at the bivouac at the moment when it dissolved and dispersed. The workers were unsure of where to situate themselves, and searched their surroundings for clues. Without the pheromones put forth by their queen, they were shiftless. She was heartbroken by all those broken hearts.

The two of us, Felicia and I, had sat on the porch waiting for her, smoking, sipping our beers and thinking the same unspoken thing—that this was the end of our uselessness, because Alicia—the innocent one— had been bitten by the *terciopelo*. Now was the end of our uselessness, because we would have to seek out and care for that innocent one, in the moment of her dying. She saw the snake, she marveled, she recoiled, she recoiled too late. And he reached out and garbled her mind with pain. Between memory and the shadows of things to come, the snake draws a thick line.

In Alicia's death I saw, as Felicia ran out to meet her, the outlines of the aftermath being drawn. No more diagrams, no more family trees. No more study. Just the blue and incredible light of morning—and Felicia in it. Fed up with sorrow. Naked—because we would need to sweat out the sadness with our whole bodies. We would get very close to poisoning ourselves with aged rum. We would think of the lost one and why we did not tell her—

But she is not dead, not yet, and the snake still lurks everywhere. The parlor game of the future marches on. Felicia and I accompanied Alicia to the site of the lost colony. I brought only one beer. That is what I thought about, the whole time. Not the girls. Not observation, but my failure to be drunk, my neglect of my own mental state. Alica's tears were tattooed across her face.

(You and I. We cried all night, once, in a cabin high in Monteverde, over the fact that one day we would each go to a place where we would not be able to find each other. What would we do in that endless underwater nightmare? The putative reason for our shared lament was that you were shipping off to Paris the next day. Had I known you were the only one who could raise my emotions to such heights . . . what should I have done?)

We spent so long staring at the lost colony, and I was so wrapped up in my desire for a second and a third and a fourth beer, that I pronounced the lost colony something that deserved our rare attentions. I did not use quite those words, but the feathering of Alicia's self esteem was done. And when we arrived home, she stayed up late at the lamp setting down her observations. Felicia and I discussed the organization of a genus of tachinid parasitoids being studied by the Canadian biologist Folles (a dear friend of mine but a teetotaler), and we drank the gallon of beer that had managed to be cold at that moment. A deluge began—a true wild rain of the wet season. The rain came down in swimming pools, in fire hoses, in continuous roaring sneezes, in drops the size of one's fist and so heavy they sounded like hail, and the thunder rolled continuously behind it like massive stone gears in the sky. The lights dimmed and faded but stayed alive. Outside, those that could make noise did. Some howlers in the distance, the giant toads, and what sounded like seven million tink frogs, started up their engines. At intervals we heard what sounded like the roar of a mama puma. The air started to lighten and get lively. Breezes poked around the house and stole all the darkness from the mind. This is what I have dreamed about every night since I first arrived here at nineteen, and the dream itself never approaches the intensity of the reality.

15

When I went to sleep last night, very giddy and high,
I fantasized about climbing the whole of Cacao at
5.30 in the morning and arriving home in time for
breakfast. I woke up instead at 8.30 and had three
beers and a six-egg omelet and otherwise have not
moved from my hammock. I feel fantastic. The sunlight after last night's deluge is a species of gold that
does not exist for me anywhere else in the world. I
have lived years as a parrot flying at a mirror. There
is no rush. The girls are out doing my bidding. The
lost colony and such.

It is good that no one asks after my whereabouts
these days. Prince Al Waleed Mohammad bin Khaled,
my Saudi benefactor and the anonymous endower of
my chair, speaks English with difficulty, and then only
with a lisp. He sends me biannual handwritten letters
asking for reports. I can't imagine answering. Once in
a blue moon I send him pictures of jaguars. He shows

them to his eight wives and, I assume, they all declare me his best investment next to the Pierre Hotel.

I am suddenly of fragile stomach, but it feels like more of an awakening than a weakness. The ancients believed that the mind lived in the guts. Down here, the standard diet, rich in rice, does not lend itself to mental fluidity. I once was host to a British tourist who happened to be a member of the retinue of Prince Charles. After ten days of touring, she lifted her shirt and showed me her belly. "I have not yet gone to the loo," she said. On her face was written the utter inability to cogitate further.

Here at the shack, I try to keep the cooking rational. There is a staple of rice, but only for the purpose of trucking flavor. We are heavy on the avocadoes and the eggs and the peppers and onions, and we are heavy on mangoes and papaya and raw vegetables. Hacienda Naranjo drops off extra produce for a small fee. The girls seem to be satisfied with the result. At least, I do not sense that anyone is laboring in vain. From what I can tell, Alicia makes well formed sculptures, and Felicia makes an alcoholic's sticky tar. Both of them are in and out before one has the chance to worry. Me—mine doesn't seem to stink anymore. At least, I can't smell it. I think my guts have gotten tired of the fireworks, given up the charade. On days when I eat nothing, weeks even, there is healthy activity. And after feasts, there is a reciprocal famine. So—too—it goes with my thoughts. When I am feeling strong, they do not come. When I have been strung out to dry and left for dead, when I have been denied even a taste of indulgence for days and days on end—and even lost my desire to have anything turn around for the better—or when my brain is shot through the temple with a hangover—that is when the machine turns over and starts to fire.

Is evolution a farce? Are we not reaching higher but lower?

Is freedom an apt replacement for bondage?

Are these things interdependent?

Is there ever a "last woman"? Or is there only a "first woman" with many faces?

Is there a way to undo something that has already been done?

What is the nature or purpose of thought?

Is it necessary to have nature or purpose?

I dream of a time when I will have rolled back these questions to their origin, their common root, and answered that one. Then—I will sit like a buddha until I levitate. But I will likely go on dreaming—of what?

I went out by myself today, when no one was looking, to find that lost colony. I took three beers. Did not find. Was interrupted by a premonition that made me stand in the forest at a certain spot. That thing you wait for, she said, you don't want it to come. It isn't what you think, said the sun. And those things you need, or think you need—your status, your intellect, your sanity, your sense of where you are located and in what direction you are headed, hands, feet—and I looked at them as if they were seaweed clung to the side of a salty vessel—they too can go, and you can stay here with me, said the light.

I lit a cigarette. I drifted. The puzzled designs on the ground led me around. I moved not with myself, but with them. After a while I had a phase change, and I bumped down the mountain slopes and into the ocean. I took a mysterious route that followed riverbeds choked with chalk blue waters. Pelicans and beetles and sulfurs were everywhere. I slid on my back down the waves of earth, and at the same time my mind found itself breathing in the cool liquid.

That feeling was one moment. Then I had a phase change again. I sensed what you might call islands of incipience in the air. The impression of something on its toes, waiting to come into existence. I saw these islands everywhere, as plentiful as the strokes and dabs of color that formed the picture. Each of them pulsed as its own heart and body and was inundated by the sea of islands around it. I shifted my gaze. A new object occupied the center of the universe, and around it swirled a new infinity.

I came home late for lunch. The girls are on siesta, I can hear them breathing like two small steam engines. There is a husk of a rotting avocado on the counter, there is the residue of a papaya, and there are skins of tomatoes. The wind begins to cool and to let slack my sails. I am laying here naked and hairy and hot. The sun is still hovering up in the nowhere. After last night's deluge, there is the first attempt at emergence. The stream dwellers (the blue bat *Morpho*) start wandering out into the light. Certain waves of certain mothlike butterflies (early *Bungalotis*) start to emerge from their chrysalids. Certain migrants who spend the dry season upland (*Xylophanes*) have somehow smelled the rain. The air is now a thick paint of sound, as if it were intended not to be breathed but to be observed from another element.

Happily, I understand less of this world than I did when I began studying it. I have picked up a great many threads and found that they are woven of filaments far more intricate and elegant than I could have imagined. But I have also found that there is far less order and reason to nature than I could have possibly fathomed as a young man. It is not simply entropy, or "chaos". Chaos has its own rules that are too simplistic and lazy to support the wonders unfolding here. Underlying life there is logic, yet it is far less the logic of evolution than the logic of an artist painting a self-portrait of himself in a room full of dancers. There is I, and there is this stingless bee (*T. fulviventris*) come to frolic in my room. We are both in the same boat of time. We are both given to appreciate certain forms of beauty. Those forms intersect in the sugar I added to my coffee just a moment ago. And we will both meet our end—I by a cancer or some ablutionary miscarriage, he by old age or the assassin's needle. Who is more evolved? I refuse to say. And I go further: there is no such god damn thing.

I and the stingless bee—we are also both in the same boat of desire. His is a bit more of an uphill battle—he is confined to the Queen. Yet I wonder if he has any sympathy for my situation. I am confined to my two assistants, half-naked in their shared siesta just on the other side of this wall. We are both victims, in other words, of a limited imagination.

One of them stirs, stretches, walks to the shower. My body is as hot as melted wax. My nerves have given up telling me whether or not I exist.

16

—

What happened next I will humbly relate. I fell to my hands and knees, knocking this notebook and my tin cup of coffee from the bedside table. The *fulviventris*, I imagine, beat a whirling retreat. The concrete floor began to oscillate. I soon realized that I was not in amorous delirium at all, and that something else was going on. I cried, "Earthquake," and I and the girls, in varying states of dishabille, flew out of the cottage. I flailed about and fell to the ground, which curled and wheeled around me repeatedly. The shock waves did not affect the three of us in equal fashion. Through my garbled vision I could see that the girls stood all but stock still, very upright, far too upright and still. They appraised me, they purified themselves in the midday light, and they changed places with one another and with so many other permutations of "woman." I tried to reach for those images, they melted away. I tried to stand. It was unwise. I dropped back to my knees. The reality of my predicament hit me when the generalized nausea one experiences in a tectonic event coagulated in my guts, and I was in dire need of evacuation out both ends of my body. I weaved myself into the brush and scrub, for shame, for *verguenza*, and blasted away no doubt within earshot of the entire settlement.

The reaction was immediate. Flies, mosquitoes, buzzards, lizards, beetles, termites took me for a goner. Six more times I emptied myself on the ground, each time more absurd and no less copious. My ears began to ring, rifling a causeway through my brain. Then I had dry heaves out both ends. A couple of times I barked out loud from the pain. My face twisted in its most extreme expression of fruitlessness, then untied itself. Enough.

I walked inside, unmanned, unhumaned, and I hosed myself off in a feverish shower. Alicia was standing in the kitchen. She had just finished showering herself (how had she beat me to it?), and her hair was an aqueous silver. Her lips too were wet. She was staring at her hands, in which rested a cup of tea. She stretched it out to me.

I am stricken with a parasite. The girls took the truck to town to pick up some pills, which are many times more poisonous than the parasite, and thus might incline me to shit out the dead husks of the demons. There is time to reflect. I reflect, that if I can only have one of them, I want it to be the one who is *sans amour*—the one who is debauched and deranged, and cold. That is always my fantasy. To get through an affair without having the colossal weight of love itself on one's shoulders. I have found that my fantasy plays out in exactly no cases. What happens is that everyone ends up being strung out over the thinly vaporized abyss of insanity.

Alicia—Felicia. Where did they come from? They did not sprout out of Harvard Yard. I never employ assistants from my university—I tried for several years, and gave up. They are too precious, too fragile, too lazy, too bookish. These two are from Michigan. They are doing their PhDs under Carrie Fowler, who is even scrappier than me. She once sat still under a tree of howlers for a month. She didn't eat, didn't drink, didn't utter a word. She discovered in that month three primate behaviors new to the field—and when she returned to Santa Rosa from her outpost, she had the incomparable humility to ask me (who had been drinking and smoking and pinning moths that whole month) to join in the publication of her findings and lend it my bearded *gravitas*. Like their mentor, Alicia and Felicia are awed and blown away by each sighting, each wild moment, no matter how fleeting or seemingly insignificant. They allow themselves to get ideas without investing their egos in any one conceit. I respect them for their academic bearing, their intellect, their willingness to run experiments in a ceaselessly changing laboratory.

I want very badly to help them—to give them space and time to pursue their own hypotheses apart from my ridiculous ambitions to unpack the psychology of the forest. I want to give them freedom to travel this country and to discover its mysteries for themselves, without the avuncular weight of my presence always upon them. I want to be an inspiration and a guidepost to them, a patron even, bearing in mind that no naturalist has ever derived benefit from being coddled. I see in them the possibility of advancing our field—the field of unveiling secrets—a painstaking and relentless task of watching, counting, and keeping time. But all I really want to do is fuck them. And I desperately need to get it out of the way, before it kills me.

They returned. Alicia brought in another cup of tea, and she brought the pills. Tapeworm you take one. Giardia you take three. I've never taken two. And if I have tapeworm, I take three anyway. The tropical gut requires a delicate balance of flora that takes several months to develop properly. During those months the old flora and the new flora wage a colonial war. Sometimes there is a stalemate, which leaves a power vacuum in which parasites do thrive. When Alicia was in the room I was convinced that my sickness was an emanation of her sex. She has grown accustomed to a loneliness in the world, which I have known to be sweet. Her movements even seem to communicate that she has a taste for what might be called brilliant emptiness—when the mind quits communicating with the body and leaves it in abeyance between dream and nightmare—between innocence and disillusionment—that state we call enlightenment.

I think Alicia is at most twenty-one years old. I ascribe to her, due to her ultraviolet beauty, a spate of characteristics new to the human psyche. Meantime I shiver with fever at every breath. She brings me more tea. She offers to take up my work for me tomorrow. I tell her that we—the novice and the ageing biologist—have nothing out of common. We are of the same mind—an equilibrium of the saintly and the profane. She smiles.

17

Next morning now, and I am no better. The appearance of things is more liquid and more transient. I have the bite of scavenger birds on my tail. I forget what it is like to be young—my fight is all flown out of me. If they knew my thoughts—these two—they would leave me hanging from the mango tree by a hundred fishhooks.

I want to empty myself. I have voided seven times today already, and still the core remains. I feel it caught up exactly in my middle. The core feels like all that has happened in Cambridge. My body is trying to rid me of all it saw and felt there, and it is failing with spectacular aplomb. Gaslighting. Schedules. My wife's voice is hollowed out by hatred, and her fat behind keeps getting fatter. These are luxuries of the kept woman—infinite resentment of her keeper, and an infinitely amorphous ass. The dumb walls of my office, where they pay me to feel important and keep quiet. I make myself wear socks that give me the feeling that my woolen pants are clinging to my calves—probably the worst feeling in the English language. Civilization is a parade of the worst feelings known to the English language. Even drunkenness, in civilization, no longer feels good at all. We sit in our salon and listen to millionaires. I myself, miserably, am one of them. My book on the humanoid behavior of bugs sold far too many copies. There was a movie, a speaking circuit, and even a children's book. My wife buys fresh everything every morning and gives the old everything to the nanny. The nanny herself is well off. She raised my two sons and we kept her on, in order to pay for her entire life. The nanny's husband is a bit of a loafer. But he has a good moustache—something I could never quite achieve. And he has the patience to fish for hours in the Charles River, standing stock still. He would be a great naturalist, but for the fact that he is illiterate.

These material things, these repugnant things. They help me in that I have much to shed—as if I had ninety layers of skin. All this shedding gives me the repeated sensation of nakedness, at very little cost. I might even peel myself down to the final layer. This sort of writing seems to be a way to expose myself without as much effort as before, when I hid behind numbers as my faithful representatives. What did they represent, for me? They largely represented my desire to be regarded as a serious man. What is meant by serious? How does one transcend birth, smile, sigh, metamorphosis?

Let us remain in Cambridge for a moment longer. In the mornings, before I go to spend my day organizing imaginary archipelagos in my mind and waiting to escape to the Tropics, I am made to focus on my breathing. I listen to an old cassette tape from the eighties, in fact, called "Slipping into the Vortex," by Auren Johnson. Auren was a guru of the Vedic faith. He tells me to let go, to let go, to let go. He tells me to forget all the things I've done "wrong", and to rephrase them as part of a natural process of experimentation. And he is right. I cannot return to my sons' childhood—the damage of my absence is done. And I cannot roll back my marriage to a woman who values respectability above all other things—even truth, even kindness—even life. I can apologize—to them and myself—but apology is a curiously meaningless exercise when held up against the mirror of time. I cannot undo what I have done to you. I cannot undo anything—so I forget. I am not particularly good at it, which is why I need to listen to Auren Johnson every morning.

What even the gurus did not figure out despite so many millennia of meditation on the human condition—and I think this is one reason why they all end up sitting so still, throughout their lives—is what I am supposed to *do* with the blank slate of my mind once I have emptied it. What my body tells me to do—even in my feverish state right now—is to seek out the one thing I know will pay dividends. Pleasure.

The word is not merely a species of activity—it is at least a genus, a family. There are high forms and low forms, and then each mode of activity has its own spectrum. What I am doing right now has the potential to exist among the highest forms—to the extent I am brutally honest. At the moment when I fashion this journal to suit my own vanity, I have lost the thread. High style, high self-image, high aspirations, all must go. Scientific research has its own dose of what I might call good karma associated with it. To the extent I can give a student, or colleague, pleasure by helping them to see a problem in a slightly different light, I am marginally satisfied with my work. To the extent I can spur a debate to an entirely unexpected result—especially if I am dead wrong in the end—and someone younger and hungrier gets the credit—I derive an increasingly sharp spike of fulfillment from the experience. To the extent I merely advance my career, I feel like a soldier firing on innocent prisoners of war. As for the exploratory part of the research, what you might call walking in the woods and looking at things—that is a gift that has not stopped giving since I was three years old. Probably my dirtiest old secret is that I've constructed this whole fiefdom around myself—all the hype, all the funding, all the lives and careers, all the conservation land—so that I can walk in the woods by myself and not be disturbed. It may not be the most refined, the most sophisticated, or even a comprehensible form of pleasure, but it is mine. When I am outside among many things that are alive, I feel I have been placed here for good reason.

What is universal does not require explanation. Suffice it to say that the gurus, including Auren Johnson, have not quite been honest with the world yet. Very well. Who has? Honesty without vanity has barely been attempted. In Cambridge in the mornings, I focus on my breathing. Sometimes, I must admit, I do not put in a great deal of effort, and my breathing becomes labored. It becomes labored with knowledge of the carnage that is to come. The weight of even a single human encounter nearly suffocates me. I shower. My body appears in the mirror as a bloated alien. There are whole precincts I would disown if I could.

After showering, and then again when I come home from work, I spend a great deal of effort trying to avoid my wife. Work, when it happens in Cambridge, is often an elaborate scheme invented for no other purpose than to avoid my wife. She has complaints regarding the placements of things. She has fly swatters. She has stacks of tabloids by the toilets. She has a moral compass. My sins are the blooded tears streaming down her fat cheeks. She has said so. I have even spent whole years of my life believing her.

How can a giant among men be repentant? How can he cower so, in the shadow of a woman? What did he do wrong (or right)? If I were reading this journal many years from now, I would ask myself this question. And I would need to go back to my thirties to begin to answer it. My early thirties—it was the early seventies. I had published my PhD dissertation in *Science.* By pure luck I was given a research position at Harvard—one that was without compensation, but one that allowed me to live in the forest full time. The years I spent down here in Santa Rosa, in Monteverde, in Corcovado, in La Selva, in the Talamancas, in La Amistad, come back to me as one long feverish dawn. I was in that brilliant stage of life when everything, every day, was new to me. I would climb halfway up the road to Cacao, or I would walk a short way down the path from Sirena, and after stuffing my pockets and a hundred plastic bags with as many specimens as possible, I would be so entirely overwhelmed that I had to turn around and spend whole days just thinking. Not the sort of thinking that was teleological. But the sort of thinking that was open ended. The mind gives the world a very large, open question mark, and the stimuli march in, one by one, like a cautious defile of leaf cutter ants in slow motion. Well, here is a theory. But there is a countertheory. And here is a potential synthesis. But there again is a counter-synthesis. And here is a principle that blows up the whole system. And here is a system that embraces and encompasses the fact that its subsystems might sometimes get blown up. And then wash the slate clean. Over and over and over again. And I would realize viscerally during those meditation sessions that I was part of it all—I could not comprehend of the whole, because I too was an animal, wandering these great expanses like a big cat just wondering what I am supposed to be doing if I am not hungry and not thirsty but nonetheless insatiate.

My heart was full. I had no possessions. I had no cares or stresses. I had two or three changes of clothing. I had a library to sustain me when it truly rained. In Santa Rosa I had a rotating harem of primatologists. In Monteverde I had you. In the suburbs of San Jose I had a Costa Rican politician's wife. And in the Caribbean I had Carlita, a Nicaraguan living with her three sisters in the Talamancan village of Bribri. I had no need of anything more than I had, moment to moment, and therefore I had no material ambitions beyond the sweet taste of a cigarette and a beer following a peasant's meal of avocados, beans, and rice, and perhaps a modest portion of very tough beef.

Sofia Martin, as she was known at that time, was a PhD student in molecular biology at Boston University.

She was married to a very small Irishman, and they lived in an uninsulated cottage on Nahant. I believe the Irishman was a telephone pole worker. Sofia had found him in a pissy pub on the south side of Boston, when she was living in a coldwater flat in Dorchester. Before that, she came from a long line of Italian academics in Padua. Her biological father was a quiet mathematician. But her mother was a drunk. She ran Sofia and her sister through three stepfathers, each less solvent than the last. After college let out, Sofia picked up and sailed to America. At the time she had scars all over her body from being burned by her mother's cigarettes while she slept. She slowly took to covering those scars with tattoos of mythic symbols.

I flew up to Boston for a conference. We were to discuss the future of genetics. At that time the extent of genetics was the idea that you could breed a horse with a donkey and get a mule. We knew nothing, yet we were starting to understand just how little we did know. There were many disciplines represented. I spoke on systematics, I reorganized one of the desk drawers of Linnaeus, to great and ridiculous aplomb. Ed Winston quantified our ignorance of the roots of human behavior. I remember him comparing our need for sunlight to that of a tree—and he got a roomful of derisive laughter. Carla Dunham said something about the sleep cycles of fruit flies which I still do not understand. And Sofia Martin spoke about the possibility of identifying one individual from another based on a shred of skin, a lock of hair, or a drop of blood, and thereby solving a multitude of unsolved murders. The same could be done with trees, bugs, and birds—the entire family tree of the animal kingdom could be picked apart. She was largely dismissed as a fortune teller. She spoke of the failure rate of juries, as measured in cases when the defendant, having been freed, admitted to the crime, or when another suspect admitted to having let the defendant take the fall. She spoke of how good storytellers can spin verisimilitude out of the most tenuous threads. And how our legal traditions were not created so much to uncover the truth as to eschew personal responsibility for having failed to uncover it. Now we had a choice, she said, we could choose truth, or we could choose tradition. The danger of choosing truth would be that once the process of justice was boiled down to a chemical reaction, the institutions of society might feel themselves challenged. And when applied to ecology, gene sequencing may desecrate our ideas of genus and species. Was it better to know or not to know?

Later on, Sofia sat at drinks with an audience of eccentrics. When I sat down at her table, she gave me an incredulous look over the rims of her reading glasses, which perched on the very precipice of her nose.

When I spoke, she looked at me as if I were speaking in tongues or Tourette's. I did not read Walter Benjamin? I did not understand post structuralism? I did not truck in Schillerisms? I was an ecologist but I did not understand the need for universal conservation? I ate meat? I drank Budweiser? I did not spend my nights awake wondering what was happening to children in the DRC? I was a dinosaur, a has-been, a half-wit, a Victorian, a Trotskyite, a flounder, a fool. I was a sort of academic philistine. Guilty of turning a blind eye to the horrors and the mass murders and the droughts and the famines and the abuses and the forest fires and the bush hunters and the suicides and the demagoguery.

All that bile, all that fervor, and all that disdain for any manufactured form of happiness or life-in-fantasy was distilled in Sofia as a curious line of behavior in the bedroom. I found this out late in that first night of the conference, following a ridiculously drawn-out negotiation. It is not atypical for a woman to want to define the outcome of a relationship before she has even had a taste of the beginning. But this round of interrogation was particularly bruising. How old was I? How many partners had I had? Had I ever been married before? What was my blood type? Had I ever slept with a prostitute? What did my parents do? What did their parents do? What was my view on children? Did I understand we were about to commit *adultery*? It was so exhausting that I was on the verge of losing interest, especially when she started rattling on about the integrity of her husband. I got up as if to leave and get myself at least a modicum of good sleep. But Sofia barred my exit. She turned off the light in her hotel room, which made it unseasonably dark. And she did something rather radical, for the time period, so far as I can remember. She fucked me in the face until her own fruition. Then she opened the door to the blinding hallway and slammed it behind me.

The impression I had, sitting wasted and shattered on the plane back home to Costa Rica, was that I had been intellectually raped. Not raped with respect to the mind, but raped physically, in an intellectual manner. A measure of force and authority. And the sense that the entire operation, from lecture, to negotiation, to imprisonment, to expulsion, had been premeditated and practiced. And the psychological discoloring that followed. Deep in the crux of other women's bodies, I began to feel a pang of guilt. I took, or mistook, this guilt for devotion. A few days after you left Monteverde for Paris (never to return), I wrote a letter to Sofia Martin at Boston University, attempting to prevail upon her to renounce her husband.

No answer came for quite some time. It was not that the post was primitive—the Costa Rican postal service had been founded a hundred years earlier, and though it used (and still uses) an antiquated address system—I was at "400 mietros (mas o menos) antes del campo de futbol de Quebrada Grande"—everyone knew, at that time, where everyone else lived. More than that, everyone seemed to know where I was at any given moment—not out of maliciousness or a tendency to gossip—but more because I was a bit of a curiosity. For a foreigner to know the forest in any intimate sense implied the intervention of necromancy. So—I thought—it was not that the letter was mislaid or misdirected. It was that Sofia Martin did not give two hoots about a bearded biologist who also did not seem to have any money, and who was prone to hallucinations in utter sobriety, in broad daylight. I carried on.

18

Day three of my convalescence. I am desiccated, weak, febrile, vulnerable. I felt Alicia touch my head this morning when she brought me tea, and I heard Felicia squabble with herself in the neighboring room, in some form of angst or jealousy. It is the beginning of the end for these two, and I am raging to get back on my feet. But I would rather feign a drawn-out malady in order to better witness their attitudes, and to finish this particular passage.

In the weeks following my realization that Sofia was not going to respond, and in the suffocating void left by your absence, I began to distance myself from my harem of Italians. Over ten days of painful abstinence, to which there was one very drunken and very impassioned exception involving climbing through the same window four times, I succeeded in winning my solitude by inducing every last primatologist staying at Santa Rosa to hate me through and through. Refreshed, I focused my energies on Carlita.

To understand what it truly meant to focus my energies on Carlita would be impossible for a creature of the twenty-first century. I would need to take that creature back to the Puerto Viejo of the Seventies. And you cannot go back to the Puerto Viejo of the Seventies. Not because you cannot travel through time, but because the Puerto Viejo of the Seventies did not exist. It was more remote than an island. At least an island may be accessed by some means. But Puerto Viejo was landlocked by impassible mountains and impenetrable rainforest on the Talamanca side, and protected by impassable reefs on the Caribbean side. Therefore there was no way in and no way out, except by bush plane. The pilots in those days flew a stripped-down version of the De Haviland Beaver. They would hook north of the central mountain range and out over Lake Nicaragua, to avoid the gales and downdrafts that whipped over the volcanoes in an hysterical and indecisive miasma. From there they would trace the canals of Tortuguero down to Parismina and Limón, and the plane would waft out over the banana plantations and oscillate like a baby in a cradle all the way down the coast. From our vantage point we could see the broad brimmed hats of the banana farmers flutter and bow, we could see the trains lined up at Bananito Sur to haul away the fruits of their labor, and we could see the boats being loaded at the port of Limón. We could see the workers' skin and their smiles sparkle in the sun. We flew through fragrant columns of smoke given off by brush fires and refuse fires scented with hardwoods and palm fronds. Then the last of the plantations dwindled, and things opened up again. South of Bananito Sur there is a long strand, maybe fifty kilometers, of uninhabited, untouched jungle. You can see in the distance the long arm of Cahuita and the mad currents trying in vain to make sense of it, and beyond that how the Talamancas march southward, and at the final moment, at risk of disappearing completely, they take a swift left turn and walk straight into the sea. That point where the Talamancas drown, and the coastline takes four last looks over its shoulder before it disappears into the forests of Panama, is Puerto Viejo. The four last looks are the old port itself, Punta Cocles, Punta Uva, and Manzanillo, and they create a set of arcs that remind you of the sails of a gigantic ship. If the winds were relatively calm, as they were in the early morning, the pilots would land directly on the beach at Playa Negra, just north of town.

I now get into a description of how my grant money from the National Science Foundation was actually spent. At that time only about ten percent of the species in the New World Tropics were superficially identified. Of those ten percent, a minute portion, perhaps three hundred, were fully described, and next to none were understood from an ecological perspective. My Costa Rican forebears had been diligent beyond reckoning, but so many of their findings were locked away in the Spanish language, and my narrative of untold mystery and the potential of miracle cures worked wonders on government functionaries in Washington who ate from hermetically-sealed plastic containers and washed their hands every time they touched their private parts. And the added mystery of a place that received five meters of rainfall per year, had no electricity, and was walled off from the world by a mountain range, was even more compelling. So, when Mr. John Kelly, a Dartmouth man with a housewife and two children living in Tenleytown, reviewed my grant applications, he always called me and asked me if there was "enough there to make your way sufficiently into the impenetrables". I would scratch my head audibly, I would sigh, and I would yield to his hundred percent markup of my cost estimates. Hence the flights, the cabin, the wine, the guaro, and far more were courtesy of the United States Treasury. What was this "far more?"

Carlita would ride down to Playa Negra at daybreak from the forested plateau of Bribri. She would arrive in full safari uniform, with pencils and field notebooks stuffed in her breast pockets and collecting bags strung from the saddles and giant butterfly nets whipping in the breeze like flags of unnamed nations. We would greet each other with perfunctory professional courtesy, and would hold up the act until the plane sputtered away into the deepening blue and we had ridden through the town and south over the rocks of Playa Chiquita and onto the long crescent that stretches towards Manzanillo. My bungalow was hidden in a copse of palms at the crux of Punta Arrecife. On the road to Arrecife, just in the shade of Punta Uva, there was a fisherman's rancho where you could trade specie for coconut milk, coffee, pineapple, bananas, papaya, and any number of incredible fruits of the sea—giant lobster and octopus, wahoo, parrot-fish, urchins, conch, grouper, red snapper, and the forbidden dolphin ceviche. Our ritual was to let the horses roam down the beach and to prepare an open fire in the yard where we would cook our breakfast, and in the meantime take ourselves out to the point for a swim and baptism. From Arrecife you can see down the whole bay of Manzanillo and into the nameless places of Panama, and you can see the sequential mountainous peninsulas to the north all the way up to Cahuita—their topographies line up like emerald curtains elevated over the sea. Not a speck of human development was visible when you looked back at the jungle from the water. Parrots screamed and monkeys howled. Toucans snapped their beaks. Smoke rose here and there in worshipful columns.

Carlita would strip naked. Her light coffee skin would blaze against the sun, so that she appeared clothed in a garment of skin-tight leather infused with the powder of diamonds. The cross of her black eyes with the black flashes of hair under her belly and arms. We levitated. We feasted. We made love. For a young native cut off from the rest of the world, Carlita had an astonishingly innate sense of pacing, delicacy, and fervor. Her communication with her own body was so pure that she could reach orgasm at any moment she pleased so long as you slowed down for her. She came in stasis, as a butterfly does in cupola, and I peeled my eyes open to behold that still-life of unvarnished climax. We would baptize ourselves again, and we would take a walk down Playa Manzanillo to Maxi's.

To a local, Maxi's was an institution akin to the Metropolitan Museum of Art—just as lively, just as cultured, just as colorful, just as essential. We drank what drifted down from Limón, and there was no question of ice. There was Stone's ginger wine, Dewar's, hot Netherlandish beer, Campari, Pimms, Benedictine's, Seagram's Seven, and every sort of nameless Rum that had ever rendered a man unable to worry about the future. The local scratch bands turned out old reggae and blues for uninterrupted sessions that could stretch until dawn. There were cripples and peg legs. There was a background of the deluge and the cackle of one-toothed laughter. There were bums masquerading as princes, and ragged courtesans paying them tribute. We would smoke homegrown cigarettes and consume gallons of firewater. Carlita would humor the old fishermen with dances, and I would sit graciously with their brothers and sisters and cousins and sons and grandmothers and admire the music and the calls of the frogs and the feeling of gentle darkness.

The nights would end, invariably, in the rain. The rain in Puerto Viejo deserves its own symphony—you have never experienced such determination and effusion from the skies. Every year Puerto Viejo receives about fourteen feet of rain on the meter, but in truth the amount is not measurable. When it rains, it rains in concerted buckets and sheets and truckloads for ill-defined and ridiculous periods, and in those periods it rains about an inch every minute. If you place a vessel in the yard it will overflow before you make it inside. It rains so hard the animals start to howl and wretch and scream and complain. The insects—those who happen to be flitting about looking for mates at that hour—are wiped out. Ground-dwelling creatures are flooded out of their warrens and driven up the trees. Spiders must take to rafting. Hollows are filled up like champagne glasses and give birth to orchids, to frogs, to odonata, to bromeliads whose hollows in turn are filled and give birth. The cycle of life brews.

There is no time of the year when it takes a breath of pause—it is constantly in heat.

We would walk the crescent of Manzanillo Beach, stripping clothes as we went, back to Arrecife, and under thick palm umbrellas into our hideaway. And we would lie naked and feel the lively air wash over us. The forest and the ocean had so much life and movement in them that they would turn our dreams into entire universes of experience. We would spend our early morning walks recounting and turning those visions about between us. Those walks scaled the steep slopes of Punta Uva and rambled through the forest of that promontory and over the other side to Chiquita and a series of hidden tide pools. The light of the rising sun was filtered through a giant churchen rose window of glass stained deep purple and deep blue, and it carved out rivers of quicksilver in the sea that followed each of us down the beach. When the tide was low we could bathe in one of the coral-ringed pools for hours, with the waves replenishing the water each half-moment. Here Carlita taught me a practice I realize I must embrace again—now that my sins have piled up so high that they threaten to topple the remainder of my existence. The practice is disturbingly simple. She would walk naked into the water with her eyes closed but facing the sun. There half submerged she would stand, hands open to the sides, still among the swelling and the gyration of the water all around her. And she would stay in that position of reception and supplication for so long that there were entire stretches of time when she would disappear.

There are no words to express the paralysis that weighed down my steps as I boarded the bush plane back to Santa Rosa. If one of the pilots had told me that I could end my suffering by jumping out of the floating plane and impaling myself perfectly on a fence post at freefall velocity, I would have been long gone. I never told anyone about my secret world on Arrecife. The act of the eccentric tropical ecologist, the intrepid adventurer, the taxonomist, the evolutionary philosopher, the towering academic sprang into motion exactly on cue, and it carried me through the ensuing weeks of alienation. The act was so convincing, even to me, that when Sofia Martin appeared on the doorstep of my Quebrada Grande cottage sporting a getup of ridiculous Casablanca flair, I took her in and proposed marriage that same night.

I awoke early the next morning in full realization that we had all—you, me, Sofia, Carlita—been swept up in a case of mistaken identity. But I went back to sleep, and the act—again—overcame me. I fear now that the act has run its natural cycle. One of these days, very soon, it must come to an end.

19

I am starting to recover. But I won't tell the girls that. I need to write this down.

Sofia had taken a hired car all the way from San Jose to my doorstep in Quebrada Grande. I had not yet discovered or colonized these barracks, and the infrastructure at Santa Rosa was primitive. So I lived in a village on the far side of the Interamerican, in the rising valley between Cacao and Rincón de la Vieja. Back then it was about a seven-hour ride from San Jose, given the mountain passes, the banana trucks, the tractors, the potholes and the missing sections of road. When she booked her flight, she had measured the distance and figured it was little different from driving from Boston to Providence. Being wildly afraid of flying, she had also consulted her colleagues for the right cocktail of sleeping pills. The cocktail turned out being so complex that it did not kick in until the plane had already bounced over the cordillera and lofted down into the central valley. Hence she slept through the entire taxi ride from San Jose to Quebrada Grande. She had just enough Spanish and just enough consciousness to tell the driver to take her to "the bearded gringo from Harvard who collects bugs, near La Cruz." Had she not been adroit enough to mention that last coordinate, she might have been taken down south to Puerto Jimenez and placed under the care of the wild eccentric James Hudacek, never to be seen again. Hudacek, one of my doctoral students, was a true genius and the hardest worker any of us had known. He had identified half the unknown species on the Corcovado lagoon. He had also worked out the ecology of a ridiculous diversity of known species, ecology that took months, even years, of dogged observation to even begin to suss out. Hudacek was so charismatic, so well situated in his personality that he would have converted Sofia, a squeamish city intellectual, into one of his obedient assistants. She would still be washing his glassware in his forest laboratory, this forty years later, and not minding the fact that the girl working next to her was bedding Hudacek on odd days when Sofia was busy fetching supplies in Palmar Sur or Golfito.

My fantasies.

Sofia had also been adroit enough to leave her affairs in the States somewhat muddled. She was separated from her husband, but not quite moved out of the house. She was divorced in theory, but not on paper. Hence I was baited with the thrill of being face fucked, again, by someone else's wife. Sofia was so passionate for release that she performed feats of sexual disgrace I have not seen (nor asked for) since that fateful week. While she slept soundly, I stood in a cold shower and wretched into the drain. I was resolved to send her packing in the morning. Yet I made sure that she had toast, fresh butter, and redolent coffee ready for her when she awoke. In her presence, which I loosely define as sexually threatening, I was unable to retrieve my independence.

I took Sofia out on a few low impact collecting trips. She was not suited to the tropics at all. A bug would flit about her, maybe it was a mosquito or maybe it was a termite or a stingless bee, or maybe it was a Sulphur moth—she didn't differentiate. Everything living was anathema to her. Once she caught wind of the presence of actual bats and poisonous snakes, she refused to leave the house. So I took her to the beach. At that time there were only only a few small hotels built on the coast of Nicoya. We stayed on a bluff overlooking Ocotal, where I knew that I was unknown. I signed us in as Dr. and Mrs. James Hudacek. I remember eating a whole lot of peanuts and reading Bulgakov beside a deserted pool. I remember swimming around a rocky point and watching the sun set into the sea. I remember taking a dark walk to seek avocadoes and having mangy dogs bark and snarl at me. I remember very little else.

I drove Sofia back to San Jose, and we spent what I felt was a passably entertaining night at the home of one of my city friends. He described how he was subdividing land in a little-known beach town called Montezuma and was going to make a killing. I told him I'd rather kill him and not see the land developed. We slept in his fountained atrium under the purple sky. In the dark of the early morning, I drove Sofia to the airport. Finally, and fatefully, in the dust and obscurity of the airport parking lot, she insisted that I penetrate her at last.

As I drove back to Quebrada Grande, there was a set of forking thoughts inside of my head, forking thoughts that have never truly ceased all these years. The first was that as a partner, Sofia was a disaster. The second was that as a wife, she could be passable, and somewhat of use to me. She had a taste for areas of domestic activity that I could not tolerate, such as spending one's afternoon organizing different species of clothing. And much of the reason why she could be passable as a wife was because she was a disaster as a partner. For one, she would never want to spend too much time in Costa Rica.

The fork of my decision was driven, so to speak, directly through my watery eye a few months later, when I received two letters in the mail on the same day. The concurrence was not so abnormal for those times, since the post was only delivered to Quebrada Grande when enough of it existed to merit the trip from Liberia. But it was certainly abnormal to receive two letters on the same day from two separate women, containing exactly the same essential content in two different languages.

It was instructive to compare their approaches to handwriting. Sofia's was made out in almost illegible scrawl, as if she were jotting out a shorthand prescription for an antifungal cream. With all of the factors that could have waylaid that letter on its way to me, she seemed not to care if I could decode its contents. Carlita's was the flamboyant cursive of a lost century, the downy supplications of a pent-up princess. Unlike her "modern" counterpart, Carlita gave me her honest emotion: she had felt since the first sighting that we were two lost ones made for each other's safety, and regardless of where my heart wandered, she was going to carry our child to term. Sofia offered to cover the cost of the abortion and disappear from my life forever.

I walked outside. In palpable symbolism, the sky was split in two—sun and bird blue over the whole span of the apron of Rincón de la Vieja and the Gulf of Nicoya and everything south, and drear and fog and foreboding clouds over the dread faces of Cacao and the brow of Orosi and points north. Everything was blowing around in a torrential wind. Cows, their ears whipping into their eyes, were huddled together in the crevices of the hills as if they were about to be shot. I took a walk up the street, towards the church and the soccer field. It was a Saturday or a Sunday, and fruits and coffee beans and fresh meats were on display in modest but resplendent quantities on the town square. I passed the market stalls, I bought a little of every-thing, and I sat down on a bench and watched the com-munity soccer game take shape.

I did not task myself with *choosing*, so much as figur-ing out how I was going to start the process of making a choice—or if making a choice was necessary. I did not even task myself with anything in particular. I was in a haze.

I spent a long time on the bench. When the game had reached its natural halftime (there were no refer-ees and no clocks, just a general sense of fatigue and good sportsmanship and thirst among townsmen), an old lady hobbled up and sat next to me. She could have been a hundred. Her cane was whittled out of a bed-post. Her clothes were an almost diaphanous cotton housedress and a pair of spanking new white Reebok sneakers. Her hair was not entirely grey—it was more pepper than salt, and tied back loosely into a sweeping ponytail. Her face was made of very fine crisped lamb-skin. Her eyes were deep, black, and watery. She spoke in a voice I can still hear, these several decades later.

"*Usted es con la nica y la gringa, si?*"

It was not surprising to me that this lady had some sense of what was going on, because it must have been written on my face that I was in pain over at least two women. But to call out my state of affairs with such particularity could only mean she was the mother of the postman, the grandmother of one of my neighbors, and the great aunt of one of the bush pilots. Such a web of close relations would not have been strange. There were only so many of us in Guanacaste, and we all felt part of the same cohort of humanity. Add to this that it was never particularly unknown what the one white man who lived in the whole proximity was doing with his hours and days, and who he was bedding. But with all the ruses and precautions that Carlita and I took, to have the smoke signal of our secret life reach all the way back up north was impressive. I told the old lady that indeed she had recognized me.

She asked me if I wanted the advice of an old grand-mother who had grown so old and rare that all she had left was the wisdom distilled from her many years toting groceries here and there and watching the people and their happinesses, and their sadnesses. She had outlived four husbands, six children, and one grandchild, who had been born without the proper collection of faculties.

I did not resist the old woman's wisdom, and I lamented the death of so many of her loved ones.

She went on to tell me, with a familiar directness that made me question if she was perhaps not an old lady at all but a reflection of my own voice, that it would do me no good to marry a Nicaraguan girl, because our children would end up half-breed bastards.

I told her that in no event would I let my children grow up bastards—that I would marry their mother straight away. And that most Costa Ricans were in effect half-breeds themselves, as the Spanish had raped and pillaged and settled a land that belonged to the Huetares and Chorotegas and God knows whom before them. And the *gringa*, as she called her, was a half-breed as well, having issued from Irish and Nordic stock that was brewed when one or another of those lands were raped and pillaged in their own time.

The old lady did not lose her good humor. Young man, she said, I agree with you that the white lady is not of the most pleasing disposition, but it is not for you to think only of yourself anymore—it will lead to no good. It is of the utmost importance that you think of your children, and what will live on in your image after you are gone under the soil and into the sky.

She went on in similar terms until she had run out of breath. I nodded, you might say profusely, and did my best to interject an end to the sermon, agreeing rather wholeheartedly that I should be thinking about my children, and at the same time thinking about my children about as profoundly as one can, when one has not yet had them, and when they are both the same age and from two different wombs. I offered the old woman a piece of the ripe papaya I was eating. "*No*", she said, and she told me that papaya tasted like dirty laundry. She told me she only used to eat papaya when her digestion was corked up. Otherwise it stripped her system of all vitality and poise, and made it necessary to ingest handfuls of dirt to replenish the flora. I offered her a few cuts of pineapple, which she consumed with relish. Finally her mouth was stopped, and in silence we shared the sundown. I did not notice the end of the soccer game, and I did not notice when she left.

I went home, and I remember feeling the sort of drowsiness I normally would have felt after walking twenty or so miles on a long and thankless collecting mission. I laid down on my pillow and lost consciousness. About forty-five minutes later (Why do I say forty-five minutes? In the moment I had no idea how much later it was...) I jolted awake in a bath of sweat. I felt unseasonably fresh, so new and reborn that the idea of sleeping again was almost pathologically foreign. I turned all the lights on in my little house. Geckoes, frogs, snakes, lizards, and moths all awoke in the cracks, the rafters, and the interstices. They all shifted, there was a flurry and a squabble, then they came to rest again. Without actually turning their heads or bodies, they all turned towards me and asked the same question, in a reptilian and lepidopteran chorus:

What is to be done?

The illusion of a choice loomed over me. I thought about the two girls in terms of images, colors, the sounds of their voices, the rhythms of their breathing. They set off against one another—I do not remember exactly how—but strongly enough that I was moved.

The night rain started to come. Giant bufos began their croaking. The freshet in the street could be heard as a cascade. I put on my boots and walked out in it.

At that time my house fronted on the road through Hacienda La Laguna. If you followed the road north, it stretched over high pastures and into the ravine that marks the fringe of the apron of Volcan Cacao. It then ascended in thick understory to a rudimentary shack that housed occasional biologists looking for a rainy thrill. The trail maxed out at the wind-abused col that led to Cacao's summit. From there it was a long and treacherous bushwack up the ridge, among cloud forest so fragile and so rare and so colorful that it haunted your dreams and blew apart images of beauty in landscapes you had cherished as a child and merged them with the meaningless and the mediocre. Coral snakes reminded one every hundred steps or so of the closeness of death.

I began walking uphill. The way was interminable. I kept going. In the high openness of La Laguna the wind whipped the rain sideways. I kept going—down into the river-frosted moat that guards Cacao's treasures from all but the stubborn and resolute, and up the terrifying slope of the river embankment to even higher pitches, higher plains. Spider monkeys in legions overhead screamed their frustration at the rain and their warning of the intrusion. An overgrown horse track sloping gradually and painfully up the apron of the mountain disappeared into the distance. A flock of *Anacrusis* moths on their evening hunt were flushed from the understory and brushed their dusky druidic wings across my face. I kept going.

I have a special nerve inside of my spine, a nerve that was probably far more prevalent in these parts before we Europeans swept up the native populations in a monstrous net of treachery and exterminated them. I go deep into the forest—where one foul step can kill you—where the sense of solitude and exposure can kill you—where a stray and famished puma can kill you—where a single thought of needing to be sheltered can melt your brains—where all odds tell you that you will not find what you are looking for—where the whim of nature is the only rule—I feel utterly and indestructibly home—I feel that the wild life surrounding me—down from the towering figs to the wasps who pollinate them—down to the last parasite—is an extension of my own body. I have never felt more panicked than those nights when I am made to lie in bed, climate controlled and swaddled in fine linens, under the slate roof of my Cambridge townhome. I have never been so calm as that night on the road up to Cacao, and I feel that every time I go out in the forest I am chasing the same symphony of solitude.

I did not get to the top of the volcano that night—it would have been a round trip of about fourteen miles and 4,000 feet of elevation. Even I cannot claim to such acts of endurance. I did reach the brow of the last high pitch before one begins to climb the staircase steeps of the final ridge. The rain let up, and the moon illumined the landscape all the way down the rippled spine of the peninsula of Santa Elena and out into Bahia Nancite. I looked down into the expanse and asked myself to choose with some finality what sort of life I was going to lead.

I decided—but not in the way that either of my "girls" would have expected. Morning, with its raw bone white light, exposed me for what I was—just another nameless thing in a world of nameless things. The things woke up and rustled their first songs and copulations. Swift trains of fog and rain came and went. I bounded down the mountain in an irrational ecstasy. And I promised myself that whatever others might do or not do, I was I. I was I and I was I. And you were you and you were you. And I was I. That was it.

The first plane I took was back to Puerto Viejo, a few days later. This time I did not give Carlita notice, and somehow, though sheer necessity, I found myself a horse to take me up the road to Bribri. Carlita was with her sisters in a very clean and very breezy little house made of indestructible hardwoods and thatch, on the bank of the Sixaola river. Her sisters gifted us a bottle of homemade guaro to celebrate our parenthood. The sisters and I drank together in the teeming rain. People peeked around the corner from time to time, to witness the curiosity. Her sisters' boyfriends arrived, and there was a bit more guaro and a primitive guitar and a measure of dancing and singing that spilled out into the rain and soaked us all. When we felt that the merriment had no choice but to end, it found a second, a third, a fourth wind. A sullen boy and his posse made their pass—it was inevitable—the jilted suitor, the heartbroken swain. I embraced him and his friends and was forgiven. By the morning the sisters had roused a priest to perform the nuptials, and the nuptials were done without particular ceremony in the makeshift audience hall that constituted the Bribri town church. Back then no papers were filed, no communique was sent to the Pope. Nor were rings exchanged—we had none. It felt like the fulfillment of a prophesy, and it also felt like the highly unlikely fulfillment of one of my most closely held dreams. Dreamlike too, in that volition played at best a supporting role in the drama. In her face I saw a distant reflection of your eyes, and that was enough.

I took Carlita on a honeymoon to the far reaches of her country. We flew to Puntarenas and ferried to Naranjo, whence we drove out to the western point of the Nicoya peninsula, to the tide pools of Montezuma and the mountain guts and unreachable wilds of Malpais. We had one of the last suppers to be had with Ole and Karen Wessberg, who treated us to an hallucinogenic concoction of rotten fruit and bitter teas. Then we disappeared up the coast, north of the Rio Bongo to San Miguel and Coyote. The beaches and the sunlight and chapparal foothills giving way to miniature mountains stretched out limitless in both directions. We got used to nakedness—there was no one around—and we became so dark that our eyes and teeth shone forth from behind our skulls like polished pearls lodged in mud. I remember sitting for hours at the mouth of an unnamed river that cut a mirrored delta over the beach, and for the first time in my scientific life I contemplated absolutely nothing. I did not think of the surroundings or their purpose. I did not think of the febrilities of my body, its wants, its terrors. I did not think of the anathema of my past. I did not think of my mother or father, my brother, my cousins, my elders. I did not think of the permanence or transience of the scene. I did not think of the catalogue of my thoughts. I did not feel the passage of time. I did not consider that I would grow old in the body or that I would become the soil after my death. I did not feel my existence or nonexistence. I did feel the cold of the river and the warmth of the sun, but no differently than a fig tree would if its roots were in one place and its crown in another.

We stayed in San Miguel six or seven weeks. Carlita began to grow round. The days bled into one another. Two fruit trees grew outside our rented cottage—a mango and an avocado—and after we tired of ceviche and turtle eggs, these two trees, and a pinch of salt, provided our entire repertoire of meals. One of the ranching families of the area operated a miniscule general store that seemed to sell only toothbrushes and guaro. From this general store we procured a deck of cards, and we passed the time playing a modified version of gin rummy between ever lengthening bouts of copulation. The burgeoning of Carlita's body and the softening of her already tranquil moods transformed the activity into a shamanic ritual that could fill entire afternoons. After the siesta we would go out to the beach and stand in the churn of the waves or sit in tide pools until the sun set into the water.

We set off for Quebrada Grande. That morning, as was my ritual, I greeted Carlita with a slow and gentle embrace, as you would a very young child. I remarked to myself, internally, deep down and beyond inner speech, that she felt *thin*. And for the duration of the drive, I was strangely out of sorts, as if someone had stuck a spanner in the works of my mind. It was entirely unconscious. My conscious self was a maelstrom of confusion over my mood—and I expressed little of it to Carlita, who was either singing, remarking on the aesthetic quality of this or that pasture or foothill, or napping, the entire drive. She had not been to Guanacaste except as a young girl, when she and her sisters had left Nicaragua following the untimely death of their parents. She found the region's serene, dusty, expansive, *gaucho* charm to be refreshing and new. And she instantly took to the flavor of what was then the country village of Liberia, as I gave her a passing tour of the markets, the central square, and some of the more quaint rural back roads, where, she remarked, she could imagine us living with one foot in human time and one foot in geologic. When we headed north and the monstrous silhouettes of the volcanoes came into view, she could not stop repeating her awe at the landscape.

The next morning, before dawn, I awakened to Carlita's screams. I do not wish to reproduce them.

20

That morning in 1975 ushered in a long period of relentless rains in Guanacaste. It was before we kept rainfall records on a granular basis, but it must have rained
nine or ten feet in the uplands over a period of three
months. The deluge seemed calculated to wash away
our anguish. Which, in a way, it did.

I was pricked out of complacency. My scholarly output became more urgent, more frenzied, and I resolved
during those rains to turn my research into a permanent appointment somewhere—even if it meant teaching bird watching to the undergraduates in San Jose. The
house was a disaster of specimens and dirty dishes, but
it was filled with the glorious clatter of the typewriter.

Meantime Carlita started her own campaign—for
the development and the greater integration of the
Costa Rican national park system. She shuttled back and
forth to San Jose and got herself appointed Assistant
Director at Santa Rosa, under a mild-mannered and

stout gentleman called Joaquin Alvarez. Together they worked towards solving the problems of corruption, defections, overhunting, cattle grazing—all issues to which I was blind back then, when our wildlands seemed limitless and beyond the point where they could ever be exhausted. Carlita went to work in a one-piece uniform that recalled a flight suit, and she grew properly plump in the hips and the midsection, as if to fill out her costume. Then one day, I felt the distance between us had grown so abruptly that I invented a drive to the pharmacy in the middle of the night so that I could shed tears in solitude. Pharmacies were never open in the middle of the night. When I got home, she was packing a bag. We did not say a word to one another. Caput.

Carlita moved in with Joaquin Alvarez, and she had five children. I still see the two of them when I have the strength to make my way into the main park complex at Santa Rosa and dine in the cafeteria, perhaps once a year. The park management is given a private dining session an hour before the biologists—one of the last vestiges of the country's aristocratic heritage. So I see them as ghosts, through a screen. When I have allowed myself to greet Carlita outside of our official capacities as administrator and scientist—perhaps three or four times over the years—she has thanked me for bringing her north to meet her destiny, and admonished me that our marriage across bloodlines was bound to end in tragedy.

21

I am now back to relative health. I went out collecting with the girls this morning before dawn. They had never been to San Gerardo, and I took them high into that rainy citadel of secrets. I was impressed at their ability to spot the minotaur in a labyrinth of color. We collected 163 larvae, two of which I do not know by name at first blush. I should reach out to Mayfield at the British Museum, so that we can discuss what is old, what is new, and what needs to be reared to adulthood. But something in me is febrile, and I cannot place the call. I am convinced that every signal the body puts forth is meaningful, so instead of fighting the demon inside of me and "forging ahead", as Mayfield likes to call it, I am going to let those two larvae remain nameless and take my assistants out to a steak dinner. I am dressed in a clean pair of khakis, and they too have taken some modest liberties with their outfits. We will see if the Bramadero still serves up a passable ribeye.

2 2

—

It is the middle of the morning, and I am probably still drunk, I cannot tell anymore, I feel extraordinarily sober but I know that this is not the case. What happened at the Bramadero and after, I will relate to this voyeur of a journal. How flippant is the arm of fate, how facile is the hand, how flummoxed is the finger? I feel that even though I have known suffering, I have had a peaceful life before just now, this night. I do not mean that I have not fucked. I have not not fucked. And I do not mean that I have not loved. I have not not loved. Nearly every human being, and nearly every creature, I love at least a little. But this combination. This particular combination in this particular attitude. And my general. How shall I put this. My general level of fitness. The degenerate feeling of my hairy knuckles against the nape of a naiad's neck. And the sight of my tumescent thorax slumped over the snowy spine of the siren and reflected in the painted glass.

What about this particular combination in this particular attitude? A man cannot know his true attitude towards a girl, nor that girl's attitude towards him, until it is far too late. It is rare that symmetry finds two people at the same time, in the same place. And if it does, fate intervenes ridiculously. One or another of the lucky victims is psychotic, or chaste, or hopelessly scarred. There are vultures, and they peck away at the union until there is nothing left but wet signatures, scripted in blood. True symmetry is rare, and it often comes too late. Here, symmetry has found us, and it is not rare at all (because the thing is thrice done), and it is not too late, because we have already gone through with the deed, from every direction and in every combination. First, it was the two of them in the girls' bathroom, while I smoked a cigarette on the distinguished terrace of the Bramadero. As I was smoking, I could hear the sound of their bodies colliding—it was like being lifted straight into a dream. I paid the bill with wavering hand—it was monstrous—we had drunk nearly a case of very old Spanish wine. All the way back to the barracks they grappled with each other in the jump seats, and I could smell the primordial scrum boiling within their bodies. I did not expect to be swept up in their slipstream—I was relieved in fact—I was horribly drunk. I kicked the *terciopelo* off the porch and hobbled to the kitchen. I splashed water on myself and lit another ridiculous cigarette. I had the nerve to pour a weak rum and water. I poured it out and re-did the drink, this time as the real thing. Somehow it revived me well enough to lie in bed and listen to the symphony. Between the third and fourth movements, my name began to be uttered. It started to take the place of certain other words in the holy hierarchy of curses. Such as:

"Jesus fucking Christ . . . James!"

Or:

"Holy James fucking shit!"

I am not even sure why the utterer uttered my name, and I do not know if the utterer herself knew why she was uttering it. For them to desire lecherous cupola with a weathered old man was impossible. I stayed put.

Yet they continued calling my name, and it was as if by pronouncing it, they relieved themselves of being eavesdropped upon and carved out a place for me in their new universe, though nominal. It was not until I heard the magic words, which I still cannot believe were issued from the mouths of one or another very young girl, that I suffered myself to enter the kitchen and pour another very tall and very neat glass of rum, and this time I entered the cold shower and was com-pletely revived. The words I spoke to myself, internally, as I pushed open the bedroom door and walked into a veritable wall of overexcitement, were something on the order of do not favor one girl over the other, or you will end up paying for it. And when I saw them tangled with one another, their two private parts overlaid in a palimpsest of pussy, the standard did not strike me as being difficult to attain. For the first hour or so, I was in and out of each one evenly, as if testing their internal temperatures to see how long they should remain over fire. In the second hour there was a mad chase of each one's tenth or eleventh orgasm. Moving into the third and fourth hours there was hilarity. There were cigarette and drink and bathroom and shower breaks. There was a very late, or very early, meal. And then in the blinding dawn we rested. I sipped my twentieth sugary rum with my balls draped over the edge of my chair. The two of them sat on the couch in the living room smoking and asking each other, through suffocating bouts of laughter, how we could possibly get any sort of work done this rainy season; or what might happen if my wife, or either of their boyfriends, were to drop in on us and smell the vestiges of sex in the house. Sex is like nicotine, it sticks to everything, it stains the fingers, you cannot wash it off, and even then the air will be tinged with it for weeks. The house as I write this reeks like the scene of a mass orgy, as if bodies upon bodies had been piled on top of one another and made to labor vigorously for their food.

The girls have identities, under their skins. One is this, the other is that, I cannot describe them yet, I need to dig deep to find the words, or the metaphors that might take the place of inexact speech. Moreover, I have digested so much of them, and they have commingled so violently with my own identity, that I do not know if I exist anymore.

2 3

This particular hangover has been faithful to the model of the most refined hangovers, in that there is a hint of pain, but far more, proportionally, pleasure in the experience of getting over the pain, and there has been a feeling of newborn fragility, in that I cannot move my head but have no desire or reason to do so. There is Schubert playing on the radio. There is nothing weighing on us. The girls have eaten the frog and visited their sites absolutely first, with nothing more than black coffee in their bellies. They returned with their notes, which are bland and unemotional and little changed from yesterday. So go the paths of love and science, entirely unrecognizable to each other. We have six colonies in production, as we call it, and two colonies that seem ready to explode or die, but the exploding or dying takes time, and for now it is a matter of watching for unknown events—a process that takes years and often is not borne out until you take your observations to the lab and run them through a machine. My machine is a French Canadian in Toronto who seems to be perfectly content sitting in front of a computer all day and playing with lifeless numbers. The statistician deflates reality like a monkey who untwists the heads of caterpillars, sucks out the liquefied innards, and discards the dead husk like the spent butt of a cigarette; the biologist breathes life back into the body and parades a phenomenon past the community in a flurry of colored balloons. The girls are swinging in hammocks outside, and from time to time I hear banter, laughter, and the cracking of cans. We are here in three-way balance, each of us equally sated and equally confused, and therefore equally happy. Yes, I might call it that—equally happy.

This is around the moment when the chronicler of one's own life should properly say that he is going to put the pen down for a while and see what he can do entirely behind closed doors. Would it be fair to abandon my journal exactly at its time of need?

The utility of questions—and their putative answers— diminishes exponentially as one gets older. Nothing *matters*, in any material sense, to the world. I guess that some things do matter to me. I will go for a long walk now and see what those things are.

24

—

We are in the very lion's heart of the rainy season, when the natural world overwhelms itself. The sky is a purple, sheltering sort of dark at midday, and it belches sheets and seas and oceans of rain down at the earth, and the earth consumes it all in a growing ecstasy of birth and rebirth. Visitations happen of the rarest beings, the ones fitted by god or chance to this environment of extremes—they form pupae when the rains are tailing off and the leaves are flying in a tropical autumn, heralding the return to six months of desert. Couched in their artfully spun teepees, in their hanging hammocks, in their camouflaged burrows, they wriggle and wait for the rains to come again. Then at once, under veil of cloud and leaf cover and impassible torrent, they emerge with their peers and, errantly guiding their flight by the light of a moon that seems all too large and all too close, they end up circumnavigating my porch lights. Many of the most spectacular bugs do not even feed—they are living off the organic material stored away by their larval precursors—they exist only for the pleasure of finding a mate and perishing—they are life and death conjoined on the wing. My research—I watched them in situ for years, I watched with an open mind and no preconceived notions of what I would find, what I was looking for, or how long it should take. The longer it took, the better—I was trying to stay away forever.

Then somehow, they awarded me the MacArthur, the Nobel, the honorary doctorate, the something-something chair, the Carnegie this, the Rockefeller that. It all made me feel that they were trying to get me to assimilate, to become part of the machine, to place me neatly on the shelf next to some other bearded fellow, to end me. Or worse, to induce me to come home and stop finding so many things out—to assume the sitting position in my office and mentor the great young scientists of the future. To slow me down. I ignored it all—I gave all the prize money to Sofia, thinking it would help. I was right for about twelve months, until she ran out of rooms to decorate. Then, I was wrong forever.

Yes—we are in the very lion's heart of the rainy season—we three—and we are deep, very deep, into the exercise of falling irretrievably in love. What began as a sport-fucking excursion has metamorphosed, has grown its wings, has taken on a new form.

And I do not care—I have told myself now that it is in vain to care about anyone or anything else. For once, I do not care if they use paper or plastic in Berlin, or if the rivers of Asia are full of human feces and industrial garbage. I do not care if there are hungry children in Budapest or Burundi, or if they are blowing away elephants by the dozen in the Serengeti. I do not care if there are riots or murders or holocausts in the streets of purblind cities. I do not care if the system goes belly-up and gives way to unpunctuated chaos. I have become unchained, unlinked to any other thing except these two. I do not care if my wife and children need to suffer for my fascination with what there is left to see and to feel in this world. I am here with these two girls—I am here with Felicia and Alicia— who represent all possible facets of joy. I do not care about the tickertape that flows through the craven ones who call themselves artists, writers, journalists, scholars, scientists, statesmen, men. I do not care what innocents cross the headlights of the lunatic at the helm of this or that great nation. I do not mean all this renunciation as any disrespect, but if you are reading this, I am dead, and it is already too late for me to care about you either.

Alicia is pouring me tea. Her face is primed into the smile of a Buddha. She touches my arm as I write this. It is only a matter of days before our little world self-destructs. At least I have left Sofia. Now I have left Sofia—after an entire lifetime I have left Sofia.

In my dreams, which have become so poignant that waking is barely a thing anymore, I have married both of these girls at one time. I have married them in parallel ceremonies in parallel bodies. I have married one and watched the other commit suicide. I have been ashamed and aggrieved. Sofia is always somewhere, watching, crying, behind an eyeless face resembling a death mask.

25

—

Let me somehow drag this chronicle into the present. The present—like a negative that has just been submerged in the fixing bath—is so much less clear than the distant past. How do I record a day, when all I can see, in my mind's eye, is eons speckled with bliss and stained by slow heartbreak?

Today, we awoke in the fragile sounds of the foredawn. We awoke in separate beds—we do not sleep together, because if we did we would not sleep. We brushed our teeth in front of the mirror. My reflection lacked its former flesh—I have walked hundreds of miles this summer—I am returned to my scrawny and sinewy Ligurian roots. We watched and waited until the coffee brewed into its metal pot, and we sat and drank it black together from our metal cups. Alicia made a light breakfast—last night's beans and rice fried with three eggs—and we cleaned our plates and each visited the bathroom in quick succession. While I was sitting on the toilet, I could see that the light outside was turning from black to purple. We walked to the truck, one by one, as each finished their ablutions. The girls sat facing each other in the jumpseats, and I drove out west—into the unexplored moonscape of the Santa Elena peninsula. Alicia we dropped off first, where the dirt track fords the Quebrada San Julio. Felicia stayed on to surmount and traverse the next ridge and drop down with me into Little Tibet. (We have been collecting bugs in this unknown bowl of wilderness now for six weeks. Our *Eciton* project is over—I sent the fruits of our labor to the statisticians to be twisted and deformed into a scientific paper.) Felicia's face, a picture of pink patience all morning, began to gather character and brilliance from the light of dawn that now burst forth in all its impossible colors. She stopped to remember something and write it down in her notebook, I drifted a few steps ahead, I waited, and she came down to me again. Her hands moved to the buttons of her shirt—she fastened them tight around her neck. She rolled down the sleeves and buttoned the cuffs. She smoothed back her black hair and tied it tight, then smoothed it back again to catch the loose strands behind her ears. She rubbed her eyes, and she handed her glasses to me to clean. This has become a tradition.

"I wish I could do this forever—go out and not know what I'm going to find. I think it is my life. I think it is my vocation. This—cluelessness. This ignorance. To see everything with new eyes. To not know."

She fell silent, and she drifted back from me again. I turned my head slowly around and looked at her. She had crystalline tears on her cheeks. I did not hear what she said next, or I don't remember exactly what she said—something about what they will think back home. The speech was muffled by her sobs. I could make out some choice illustrations of her family's wealth—her father was a guardian of an ancestral trust. She was an only child, and it would break her mother's heart if she never did come home. It would dash their dreams.

"I feel that I am abandoning them. Do you understand?"

"Happily, I do not. My parents were academics, and they were so self-absorbed they never noticed me gone."

"Mine want me to be a lawyer. Or some horrible thing like that. Enclosed in glass like a fossil. To defend our fortune."

We were collecting in Little Tibet, in the blazing dawn. Everything was alive and awake. Every sunspot was populated with a treasure.

"You are a scientist. And a philosopher."

"They think you are a crazy old man, and that you are brainwashing me in the ways of some sort of environmental Communism."

"Let them think what they like. You can never change them. You can only defy them."

We went on in this vein, and my mind gradually drifted down through my neck and into my stomach. I started to notice a remarkable heaviness in my legs and feet, and my shoulders felt like a thin wire hanger draped with meat. They wanted to sink all the way to the forest floor. My arms, in theory, would sink too, leaving me looking like a war battered Roman bust, or simply a decorative head on a pedestal. My hair would be white, my lips would be white, my ears would be white.

"I could use this fortune to reclaim most of the rainforest east of Orosi all the way to Upala and maybe even east to . . ."

I could plant that decorative head anywhere I pleased, just once, and I would not be able to move, but would not need to move. Would it be there, in Little Tibet? It would likely be there, in Little Tibet, that I would vanish into the next life.

"And we could build biological stations east of Dos Rios, in places so little explored and so little understood, and we could preserve a biological corridor so that all these creatures can find a place to go when they are burned out of here and Santa Elena is an island desert again. We would instead be walking in the Caribbean plain, with a new set of interactions to explore—just as if we were the first to happen upon this peninsula after it collided with the mainland and created this miniature California. The hills, the live oaks, the golden grasses, the two must have come from the same mother, out in the Pacific somewhere. Where islands were born."

My body felt like it would indeed be pulled underground that second. I remember a similar feeling coming over me in church, as a child. A climax came in the story, and the congregation was made to stand. I got up from my seat, and all the organs in my body unhooked themselves and went into a freefall and splashed on the marble. This was the feeling of being a nonbeliever—emptiness. I did not feel better for having that nerve in me that knows myths to be untrue, and seeks only truth though it fails to console. So too now—I do not believe that my magical macaw moth, the shocked scarlet russet-winged giant arrowhead *Schausiella santarosensis*, will find a home in Upala. That thought alone causes my skull to deliquesce and my brain matter to pool in my boots. I cannot even bring myself to write of the others . . .

"James . . . James!" she said. I had not heard her sermon, I had not heard anything about her plans for yet another miraculous life-saving stroke of grit and genius.

"James. Do you think I am crazy? Do you think my plan can work? I will need to buy up all the farms . . . I will need to fend off the hunters, the ranchers, the ragtag militias, the marauders, the corrupt politicians, the cartels, the military juntas, the ghosts and the voices of failure . . . just as you did. Just as you did! And I will need—we will need—half an army to defend such a large area. But what do you think, James? I can go home, and then . . . ."

I told her I would do nothing to intrude on her dreams, that her life was her own entirely, and that I would be remiss to impress upon it my personality, my values, my own expectations and methods.

"But seriously, James, what do you think? Can this be done again? Can Saint Peter's be rebuilt? We must succeed at this, or else . . . "

"What about the villas, Felicia? What about the villas, and the dogs, and the jets, and the ottomans, and the Dutch masters, and the waterfront lawns? What about all that? The tens of millions—what about your future children, the pleasure you will have in raising them, your womanhood, your livelihood?"

"I spit on all that, James. I spit on it."

"Well then, spit hard."

She seemed to take this as approbation—she shivered with fulfillment, she jumped into my arms and we fucked in an instantaneous fever, like two birds coupled in flight. As I inseminated her I felt the torch pass. With the last spasm—she had it in her—just as I had felt it pass to me, in a San Jose bordello, decades prior, when the working girl swiftly swallowed me in the red glow of her bedroom. I looked in her mirror and I saw in my eyes the glow of a fiery outcast. From behind that looking glass I told myself the entire story of what was to unfold, over my entire life—in one long and slightly simpering stare—I revealed to myself that I was not who I thought I was—I was far better and far worse— far more powerful and far more fearful—a being that spanned every lost corner of the spectrum of humanity. That telegram—the one that foretells the horror and the richness of your life—I passed to Felicia today. After so many years of cobbling fame around an inflated version of myself, I am without a persona. Good riddance to that man. Good riddance to the costs—the midnight maintenance costs of the myth of myself. Good riddance to the lie that dogged me in every elevator, every hotel room, every classroom and senate chamber of fallen humanity—the lie that I cared one jot about the fate of the world, that I was a selfless sort of conqueror. I cared only about one thing—and that was the freedom to walk these forest paths and indulge my curiosity without molestation or threat of personal extinction. I cared about the survival of James Santo. And now it is time for James Santo to start disappearing.

26

They both—Felicia and Alicia—confessed their love to me last night. I reciprocated—and I told them that I loved them equally and in turn, just as a frictionless pendulum will swing in perfect symmetry. That they were in an oscillating pattern inside of me like the Earth turning on its axis in space. I confessed that I knew them from another life, that their live presence in my waking world was making all meaningless questions fade away. My concrete, my exacting, my defined and definable self was flowing out of me, and the feeling of that outflow was part panic, part loss, part relief. I could not possibly feel better than I did in their arms, even if I had originated a theory that explained all of existence since the beginning of measured Time.

I told them that the rest of the season would be left to chance—to the highest form of inquiry—the one in which you do not even know what questions to ask.

We three wandered down the stream at the heart

of our Little Tibet again. Alicia found a dead fifth instar of *Rothschildia* and crushed it. Out came the larvae of its parasites. She rolled the larvae between her fingers like pearls, her face in gentle contemplation of what it must have meant to die at that stage of life—as a naked forethought. We wandered apart, each to his and her own instincts, in a shared trance that attuned our senses to the hair's breadth scouring of the undersides of leaves for differences in color or texture and for the unnamed and unknown life forms that watched us as we hunted them. I do not know what they felt during these moments—but I felt their blood, their energy coursing in me—up from the legs and gathering speed for a fantastic collision with the underside of my skull. And in turn I felt myself tossed and machined about in their arteries, trucked back by their veins and skyrocketed into the fireworks of their minds like a satellite. When I suspected that one or the other was elated—at a sun ray—at a reflection in the stream—at the cold of the water—at the mist in the air—I soared with the circling carrion birds, my wings poised in a portrait of effortlessness. And when I suspected that they despaired of their search, I lost the ability to breathe, I suffocated in air.

We met back at the truck as the sun was drawing down over the ocean and giving us its deep bloody stare. Our belts were laden with specimens, our legs were heavy as tree limbs, our faces were alive with a happiness that felt permanent. We stuffed the cab of the truck with our bags, and we squeezed into the front seat. Both girls had specimens they could not identify, and instead of rattling off the names of the caterpillars (three widespread but scarce *Noctuidae* and three cosmopolitan *Erebidae* down from Rincón), I let the mystery hang in the air. Perhaps I will let them re-name these six species—why in the world not? Who will stop us?

I want to repeat today until the end of time. Now I am consumed with ways to rid myself of interruptions—papers to write, classes to teach, a family to shelter and protect, money to raise, a world to save—I want it all out of the way. That is my prayer to whomever is responsible for this collage of sensation and illusion. Help me make room in my life for these two girls. And help this feeling not to cloy, dissipate, dissolve, or reveal itself as something else entirely.

27

—

I fear what will happen when I start writing down my dreams. The girls are speaking to me even in sleep. Their thoughts come out disorderly, unreportable, sometimes cheap, sometimes contrived, sometimes precious, but they come out. They are changeable like the seasons, they are not always my allies—they are one with their own identities— apart from me. But is anyone, anywhere, always your ally?

I no longer seek to know what is true. I seek to know the way our god or gods imagined this world should be. The truth is too humbling, too dark, too terminal. When I first arrived in Costa Rica in the late sixties, I could predict to the hour the comings and goings of the rainy season and the *veranillo*. Now there is no predictable rhythm. The rains come forcefully but haphazardly, and those haphazard rains fake millions of bugs into emergence, only to cook, desiccate, and starve them back to death. You might call the extinction, or extinguishment, of the insect populations in our habitat, the last large swath of seasonal dry forest in the New World tropics, a harbinger of the horror to come when we, too, are swatted away like lost chips by a croupier's rake. But to me, it is the end itself. Under my surface, in my universe, which is a special universe, the entire world is dying. The girls—they see a new frontier and a new vision to the East, where the rains will remain more reliable and more plentiful. In many ways I inspired their vision—I bought the land bridge that connects the two biomes, and I foresaw that someday that bridge would be extraordinarily dear—when all living things would be forced to move upland and windward. But I did not foresee how swiftly and how heartlessly the destruction in the lowlands would be carried out. Or perhaps I hoped I would not survive to see it. Mammon's fiery stream of piss is destroying the last, greatest work of poetry done by the unnamable. This last, greatest work of the unnamable—it was not humanity. It was the innocents who came before us, and we are the horsemen of the Apocalypse.

I am writing in the early morning, while the girls are still asleep. I had a moment alone with angelic Alicia last night, while her more seasoned comrade slept in the next room. There was an added pleasure to this fucking-in-open-secrecy—the half-forbidden, half-stolen, half entirely permissive feeling in the air lent our parts a special sensation. More professions of undying amour emerged from Alicia's lips. More outlandish tearings at each other's faces and chests and hair, and more openings of trap doors and false fronts inside our bodies. More breathy silence that spread the moment thin like mist over my entire life history. More discoveries of parts of the girl that do not have names but now for me have permanence.

In these quiet hours, at the ragged ends of the nights, I am visited by the cloaked ghost of Sofia. Years ago, when I would first see her after a season of collecting, she would meet me at the airport, just as if we were actual partners. She would express undue excitement at my return, she would cry with hybrid happiness. How wide her eyes, how strident her declarations of respect and devotion. She would arrange the shower for me, with new razor and tea tree soaps. A thick cotton robe would dangle from the door. By this time I would not have seen hot water for months, and with my twenty or more kilometers walked each day I would resemble a man held hostage under great duress. My hair and beard haggard and grey. I would first use an electric clippers to make the beard ready for the razor. I would watch the years fall away from my face—I am not so old after all. I would wash my body many times, and my veins would engorge themselves in the heat. Then—the feast. It would begin with shrimps and champagne, it

would end with berries and whipped cream and anis-
ette, and a final sip of espresso. My sons would relate
tales of their affairs, their travels, their business pursuits, their trials, their little victories. They would make
me laugh—they are in fact quite well humored—and
Sofia and I would gaze across the table at one another
with something approaching pride—or relief—that Paul
had not yet killed himself and had not (yet) brought
home an out-and-out prostitute, or that Simon had
not run himself to the ground with work or worry.
We would wash the dishes together—Sofia and I—and
her presence, that day, would give me a hard-on that
drained all the blood from my brain. Her beauty was
long lost. It was her weight, her gravity, that attracted
me, and her knowledge of her own sexuality, her womanhood. We would go into our bedroom, finish quickly,
and return. More espresso, more liquor, and cards. This
bright cycle would continue for about a week, maybe
less, rarely more, then our sons would go back to their
lives in Manhattan and California and leave us alone.
Maybe there would be a lag of twenty-four hours, when
I would fantasize that I lived in an alternate reality.
Then the beatings would begin again. I have wronged
her. I have abandoned her. I am selfish and vain. I
have been the worst kind of husband and devil. I have
ignored her wants, ignored her needs, I have spoiled the
marriage, I have stolen her career, ruined her life. She is

alone, so miserably and hopelessly alone. I have declined to take care of the bills, to wash the cars, to empty the trash. Grievances large and small were leveled with one another, such that a lost sock was equivalent to uxoricide, and they were then leveled then at me, in echelon formation, with inescapable fury, tactical retreat, and potent rear-guard Parthian charade. Each night I was left in a denuded Ardennes of the heart, defeated, dejected, depressed, and plotting my next act of escape. At this point she would cry, and beg for forgiveness.

I do not make an ideal husband—my needs are rooted in ideas—in sometimes fatuous and self-serving and ruinous ideas—such as the idea that my own renown will make any difference in the way humans relate to their surroundings, or the idea that with my help, a country with a budget one tenth the size of Massachusetts' could turn back the clock on an extinction event that is affecting every corner of the planet, or the idea that I could make a hair's breadth dent in the monolith of human ignorance surrounding our existence. I am indeed a vain man, and a foolish man, and even you might say a childish man. And I have disregarded, kicked aside my wife's needs in order to roll my assigned stone up the slope of my own personal hill in Hades. Moreover—moreover. Let us talk about my other qualities. In certain regards I have an iron constitution, I can drink like perhaps a more studious version of Hemingway, I can hike fifty miles without water, I can climb a hundred-foot tree with my fingernails, I can hunt snakes and bats and jaguars without fear. But visit me with a headache, or an earache, a feeling of infection, a digestive complaint, or god forbid a case of the spins, and I am as meek, as feeble, and as dependent as a young girl. However. I am not a person who delights in causing other people pain. I am incapable of violence. I am as patient and as diligent as a Trappist monk. And yet Sofia—yet Sofia. She wants to talk about my drinking. My sleeping and waking habits. The stain on the coffee table. The stain on my shirt. The stain on the seat of the car. The coffee cups strewn about my desk. The mail. The news. The larger home down the street, where dwells a banker and his constipated wife. The sink is too small and it is dented, and I have not fixed it. She could have a newer bedspread. She could have a vacation home close to the sea.

All I can think of during these speeches is the dust cloud of wasted time that will dog me until death.

Never mind—behind my Sofia, there are a billion Sofias—my only recourse is a meditative, even an artistic sadness that colors the dawn a deeper blue and the evening a deeper red—when I am here, in the wilds, where I belong. And perhaps I am lucky to have such a sadness, when it makes me so much more sensitive, so much more generous, so much more vulnerable to the two innocents just beginning to stir in the next room.

28

Alicia said to us today—I will try to remember—she said, "Do you believe that there must be a thing such as a death wish without the concomitant depression? Such a thing as wanting to unlock ourselves, to free the heart from its cage?"

"You are holding a mirror up to my mind."

"I think the more time I spend out here," said Alicia, "the less I will ever be able to return. I do not even want to speak to anyone. I do not want to get on an airplane. Please do not make me. Please do not make me get on an airplane. I want to disappear into the soil and the sunlight."

We had captured hundreds of *Automeris io* caterpillars from the crowns of three monstrous live oaks on the grounds of the old Santa Elena hacienda, and my hands were numb from their poison. The girls showed no sign of pain or fatigue. The specimen bags dropped from them every few moments and bounced and fluttered to the ground.

"No, Alicia, I will not make you get on an airplane. I will not make you do anything."

"But I mean—never, never. Do not let me leave this place—I am not fit for the world."

Felicia and I looked at each other, then we looked at Alicia. The girl's fingers were crawling with *Automeris*. She stung herself in the face each time she tried to push back her tears.

We collected until the sun disappeared. I begged off for some rest before dinner. The girls are cutting limes and grinding mint in the kitchen. I stole a drink of straight rum, thinking it would help me understand the gravity of Alicia's plea. If she never leaves Santa Rosa, does that mean I never leave Santa Rosa?

29

—

This morning, familiar ghosts roused me before dawn—thoughts of what I had not done and would never do, and thoughts of the most mundane failures—such as the time I left Sofia at a train station in Philadelphia and she slit her wrists lengthwise and nearly bled out on the platform—such as the time I offended the chief editor of *Science* by publishing a diatribe against his cousin, the famous entomologist Luther Bert, whom I did not know was related to a man with the surname Von Pozner.

What happened—I awoke in a fog and a paralysis. My neck would not nod, my shoulders would not unshrug. My eyes had a blue film over the lenses, like an alien's eyes. The light spilled virgin white over the speckled concrete, the worn wood cabinets, and the chipped metal cups of the kitchen, mocking me. I made a very slow pot of coffee, I could not complete the ceremony in due time. Alicia and Felicia stood next to me, their feet bare, their hair fanned into haloes and ribbons of filament. We waited. And someone said,

"I'm tired."

Then someone else said, "I'm tired too."

And someone else said, "We are all tired."

Two black holes formed in the soles of my feet, and my innards exited through them. Night seemed to draw down on me just as the dawn was at its brightest and most horizontal. I had horrific thoughts of Sofia and the life I would never succeed in reinventing—it was too late, and I was too scared, too silent, too much in my head—and these girls—these girls needed someone better. More to the point, each girl needed her own man, and I would not choose between them. It would break the heart of the other. And somehow at that moment I realized—this is all going to end badly. We are all headed for interminable pain, for my inability to choose at all, for my paralysis in the face of the either/or. I was about to open the rum bottle and go back to bed for ever and ever. But somebody dressed me, and somebody threw me in the car. Alicia drove—she never drove—but Alicia drove the Cruiser out to the beach at Cuajiniquil, and she sat me on the sand with myself, just with myself, and she laid her half naked body down on me and forced me to be in one place, unmoving, extant, and she did the same for Felicia who wrapped her arms around her friend and screamed like an ecstatic bird who had just found a tree weighed down with perfect fruits. The two lay compressed against one another for hours as I stared up at the cloudless sky and let the sun cook my skin. I went into the water and I came out of the water. I went into the water and I came out of the water. I went into the water and I came out of the water. My metronomic baptism stayed the dread scales of reason. The sun came down and silhouetted the water against the horizon, and it turned the beach into a rippled desert landscape spread with mercury. The water was waveless, and although tepid to the first touch it had cold undertones once you reached depth. Spotted eagle rays wrestled in the shallows. Wild cackling parakeets screamed helloes and accused one another of avarice or sloth in the trees. A fisherman emerged from his hovel in the mangroves, scooped the bay with his net for a few minutes, and came up with an armful of spottail grunt for his lunch. Two cowboys on paso fino horseback, both rider and horse in full regalia, appeared out of nowhere, then vanished. The girls went for a walk, and I slipped into a thoughtless meditation—my mind devoid of fear and expectation—and woke up—no pain, no poison, no wants, no terrors—either a few moments later or a few hours. The girls found a mango tree, and we ate a lunch of green mango and salt. We were not hungry at the beginning of the meal, and at the end of the meal we were not full. Our bodies were even, balanced, strong, lithe. We put on our boots and wore our discarded clothes as bandanas and set off down the rocky coast. The slabs and boulders appeared newly hucked from the mantle, their surfaces dimpled and jagged and by no means smoothed by the tides, and their orientations baffled and alarmed. Some slabs were stacked up like dominoes or stonehenges that had been toppled on one another in their respective sleeps. In the tidal pools formed by these accidents, perfectly painted sea snails rested, and crabs noodled and spied. We scrambled our way out of the mouth of the bay of Cuajiniquil and onto a rocky and exposed pocket beach all but inaccessible but by dropping off a high ledge by one's fingertips. There we turned our faces to the winds and the outrageous vastness and the danger of the Pacific, and satisfied with our pilgrimage we slowly, gingerly, picked our way back along the shoreline to the shelter of the main crescent and were baptized again. Somebody suggested we drive home before the dusk. The girls are in the kitchen mashing mint and sugar together once more. My malaise, my trouble, my apathy, my sense that I am repaying the debt of long-forgotten sin, all has fallen away. All but a slight shiver inside when I think of what I have left behind. I cannot decide whether I want it or hate it—the shiver is not interpretable. And why must it be want or hate? What causes me to think in such extremes? There is a black hole inside of me, and since it is black I cannot make out what is written at the entrance to the cave. "Arbeit macht frei"? "Lasciate ogne speranza, voi ch'intrate"? "Nevermore"? Perhaps I romanticize the cave too fully. Is it simply a dearth, a lack, a lacuna, with no particular meaning? How can such an integral part of one's being have no particular meaning?

So . . . so.

I can answer my own questions all night.

It is time to live, time to become lost.

Time to forget.

The most radical, the most secret power of man.

Perhaps inside of me there is a place where things go to be married with eternity.

Perhaps it is a land of disappearance.

A paradise.

PART TWO

1

I have not written in so many months, it feels like I am going to confession after having walked the streets of Bogota as a hooker. My idea of approaching the page again is a kind of uncloaking—a coming-out of the aristocrat from under the skin of the toad. It has taken me many attempts and failures to set down even these few words. For days I have been looking at the blank page and watching my watch until it is time to get drunk again. Or if I am lucky I dodge the lead tipped bullet of the rum or the whisky and go straight to the weed and benign total paralysis. The feeling of physical fulfillment is so rich that I do not feel compelled to exist. My dreams have become a hundredfold more vivid while my daily life has reduced itself to the subtlest motions. Last night, I stood on a backcountry airstrip with my bags packed—it felt that I had planned this journey for years. The sun over the treetops was the blood red horizontal light of evening. My plane was flying where my dream planes always fly—deep into Corcovado to a place that is nameless and unexplored —back in time, to when my ideals were still intact. The engines started to rattle and whir and scream. I was airborne, the tiny plane gyrated on the winds like a leaf. Below there passed Montezuma, Puntarenas, Hermosa, Uvita, Drake Bay, Sirena, Puerto Jimenez. The plane turned out to sea, and I disappeared into the western horizon with the sun. So, my dreams.

This morning, I awoke before dawn. I put the water to boil on the stove. I broke down immediately upon measuring out the coffee—four cups. I did not understand for whom this tribute of tears was written—there are too many candidates—so at least some part of my sadness arose from confusion. The other part of my sadness arose from my longing for someone so far gone—so far gone—that I do not believe I could utter your name to the page without blowing up this entire work. You are not Sofia, you are not Carlita, you are not Alicia or Felicia, you are not any of those voices that haunt me in their midnight laments. Their faces—I cannot tell you anything about their faces. It is the curse of the spurned that the lover's face is never quite right in his mind's eye. It is blown up as if exhumed from a burial or dredged from the bottom of a lake. It is rolled out and ironed flat and colored wrong like a cubist terror. The color of the eyes does remain. The voice does remain. The private parts do sometimes remain, if they stood out to begin with. If they were too perfect, they bleed into all other visions of perfection. The hands...the nails. I can remember the strength of the grasp of certain hands that touched me decades ago, and but once. Feet—some women have expressive feet—feet that tell a story. Feet with toes whose procession from fat to tiny have hiccoughs—like yours—in a sign of genetic caprice. Feet with toes that fan in all directions like the toes on a tree frog and that move like silent crickets while their owner expresses emotion. But the faces in my mind are drowned, battered, wrecked. These denuded echoes hover around me, they pass through me as I walk from chair to coffee pot, from coffee pot to chair, and every time they pass through me they exact a penalty, until I am walking about as a negative of James Santo—and from that negative the image is reborn. So the days. So the interminable nights.

In my former life as a father, a husband, a man, a scientist, I could escape all means of torture by wandering off the map into places no other man had touched, into entire realms of thought that you could not classify. Now it is all mapped, it is all digitized, it is all flown over and spied by satellites, and there is no leaving the machine or its troglodyte tantrums—the weather patterns that are turning Santa Rosa into a desert of my fantasies. Let me tell you a secret—a dread secret that will murder me from the inside . . . . Since Felicia and Alicia left, the rains have not returned. These forests were seasoned with love, and now that the love is gone, its host will vanish too. I fear. I do fear. In fact the only use of my fear is to keep the facts at arm's length—for what I have feared since the rains started to get fussy in the late eighties has already come to pass. Even Little Tibet—the streams of Little Tibet are dry, and the desiccated corpses of pupae who were seeking moisture and camouflage in those cool wet shades are being devoured by scavengers as I write this. I have even hiked to the peak of Volcan Cacao, with the sole intent of committing suicide by throwing myself off the principal ridge and into the pygmy cloud forests to rot there—and the wonderland is gone. I could not even cry in that moment—the devastation was so complete that it left nothing to cry over. I cried this morning instead, and the disappearance of my world was mixed with the disappearance of my women. Women whom it now feels I enlisted expressly to bring me to this point—to one's knees at the altar of silence—to get to the heart of what it is that I have, and what it is that I do not have, when all else is stripped away.

2

What happened? What does it matter what happened? Shall I tell you the story of the genius doomed to the echo chambers of purgatory, where he hears, for all eternity, the diatribes of his fat wife, the sounds of Felicia's vomiting in the toilet, the sounds of Alicia's whimpering, and the empty sounds of silence in the still afternoons as the wildlife perishes of famine in this lengthening *veranillo*? Mysteriously, I have no desire to die like Casanova, though my pain multiplies with every breath. How, here at the bottom of my existence, can I finally reach skyward, or is it inward? How, at the height of my dolor, can I seek not the morphine but the trouble itself—and the trouble to deracinate. How, in other words, do I get out of this alive? I feel that if I touch the rum bottle I will never make it home again—home being where? For the first time since god knows when, I feel that my mind is becoming unhinged from the desires or stage directions of its host—fully present yet at the mercy of the prevailing winds of existence. We speak of the actions of animals as if they arise from pure instinct. There is no animal volition. What, then, does a human feel when driven by pure instinct? Is it something akin to this sense of buoyant terror? There is no intent in this letting-go, it is more a being let go—like a balloon released from the hand of a child, to extend out into nothing. So I have come unhooked from myself. I am free. Freedom.

3

I touched the rum bottle. So be it. The worst thing that can happen is that I fail to wipe away my aspirations. My father was content to have a wife, a home, a family, a profession. I do not know where this restlessness came from—this urge to be first in some unknown—and it has landed me here, in a barracks off the Interamerican, alone in the thickening heat and destruction, my methods of human presence in the wonder of nature all but fossilized. And still—and still the restlessness burns. I am fit to jump out of my skin—in fact the skin seems to want to detach itself and costume another being, for this one is done and pickled—I do not know if I can remain here and bear witness to the slow unraveling of my dreams. It is so hot I can barely breathe. I can feel in my viscera the world being pushed off a cliff and accelerating down into the void. A trapdoor opens up in my chest and my whole being is sucked in and down into the galleries of the underworld, where there is yet another trapdoor and a world darker still, beneath.

I cannot go to Little Tibet. Little Tibet is gone. I fear I might rail at the skies and castrate myself out of blind frustration.

I heard reports from Jorge Villacorta that the forty known capuchin monkey families in Santa Rosa have lost all their young, and that the reproductive organs of even the most fervent of the alpha males are shriveled and grey. The morning forests are becoming eerily, ridiculously quiet. The sunrise, the living world's worship of the sunrise, is the most exuberant, the most fantastical, the one event, the oldest tradition . . . .

I touched the rum bottle and it does not help, but I touch it further and deeper. I feel my body is fighting the drink. The two are in a bare fisted boxing match for my soul—it will it be a fight to the death—unless I can manage to bring in a third party to stop the action.

A dream. I just got the image of a dream. Three girls, in three, how do I call them? Alcoves. The one does not know of the other. They are each . . . how do I say? Skeptical. They belong to me, they are in my dream, but they want me to prove something to them first. They want proof of my love for them, which they demand to be given in the form of the dismissal of the other two.

I laugh, I demur.

There appears a magic bus. A school bus outfitted as

a mobile bordello. But classy. Very clean. The blinds work like a charm. The bed is spotless but for a single drop of blood. Someone is behind me—the girl who suffered herself to be one of three—and became one of one—her hair is black and her eyes sea green. She declares her undying devotion—and her nipples drop into existence like pale pink marionettes. At this moment we are exposed. Sirens wail. The authorities board the bus. Sacre bleu—we are parked illegally. It is always some mundane worldly impediment that gets in the way—and then there is the small technicality of all this being a dream—what is one to do about that?

Find your anchor, your chief metaphor, in your actual past—is all the psychologists can muster. But I am a student of nature, and out here, the life forms I study do not have pasts. They crawl, they eat, they *metamorphose*, they fly, they mate, they die, without teaching each other anything, without the time for encounters with any sort of meaningful living history. They are pure expressions of the stream of consciousness of the universe. So—and so. What are we? If we are imbued with the gift of sight and hearing, why not say that we are imbued with certain memories of who we were generations ago—and the history of our species provides the substance for our dreams?

Three girls—and the question strikes me—am I equating myself with these three women? Is my worth determined by whom, in the end, I choose to lay with? I dream about my possible wives. Each of them wants something from me. But what do I want from them? Do I want anything? Why do I inundate myself with their cares? The intimacy of a place. The expense of a thing. Ineffable ardor and such. Terrible happenings and their universal application. The appearance of the self and her universal application. The gravitation of the moon and the gory consequences. The taste of food. The cleanliness of one's person and attachments and surroundings. The fight against time and the striations it leaves as it drags its fingernails across our faces and down our chests. Children: the future. The future that never comes—the ribbon of fear stretching out ahead of us—a wife is not paid, so to speak, to live in the present, but to dream up all the possible consequences of the original sin of existence. Politicians—credit card companies—the tax man—bacteria—bullies—radicals—vermin—they've got you in their sights. Every so many years Sofia and I would enter pitched battle over whether she ought to murder an innocent moth who had mistaken our kitchen chandelier for a hydra-headed moon. Fear of rape and kidnapping by the hand of the darkness itself. Fear of the future judging them second rate, and not bothering to rape or kidnap them at all. Fear of nothing happening. Fear of something not happening. Fear of things or places without names.

Fear of infertility. Fear of poor people. Fear of honest people. Fear of peace—for peace gives rise to the anticipation of conflict. All these narrowly concentric cares are toxic to the intellect—the intellect has little tolerance for noise, for the clatter of pots and pans and high heels. But I seek women out—in the sanctity and freedom of my dreams I seek them out—they are my last buttress against the yellow eyes of death.

One night I was in Mass General very late. Never mind why—there was no why. I drove myself to the hospital in a moment of deep suspicion of my existence. But never mind why. The hallways of the emergency ward were strewn with grey-skinned patients. One—a very old man who had evidently suffered a stroke or a hemorrhage and was awaiting a surgeon—was screaming with pain all night. He was screaming like a child who had shoved his finger into a wall outlet. Perhaps that is what death is—electrifying. At some point he fell silent, and they pulled the curtain closed around him. Always—always behind a veil.

The history of our species—the substance of our dreams. The explanatory power of language fails at the threshold of human experience. Because describing a vision or a sensation gives me little insight into how to deal with it. That girl who followed me into the bus, was she the right one? Or was her very presence a lacuna in my judgment, a frivolous oversight? Black hair, green eyes: Sofia. But not the Sofia of my failed marriage, another one. A younger, more resolutely beautiful girl, and firmer in her belief in herself. One I have not yet met. The dream is telling me there may yet be another chapter to my life—that there is something to wait for— that the youth has not left me entirely.

After the dream of the three alcoves and the magic bus, I had another one. My whole extended family, living and dead, is at a very old hotel in what feels like Paris. Bellhops and servants are everywhere. Red on the floor, brass on the mantles, firelight flickers against an ornate plaster ceiling. I need one thing—to take a shower—but the showers are all out in the open, grotesquely display- ing bathers caught soapy and unawares. One of those bathers is my sister—and her eyes cast a licentious gleam as she pushes her breasts together so that the nipples almost kiss. I feel a pain inside of me, a sense of pure wrong—and I spend the rest of the dream—what feels like hours—trying to escape the hotel. But all of the streets leading from the exit are linked to another wing of the labyrinth, another set of bathers on display, another replica of my sister with the indelicate eyes of a cheaply fictionalized whorelet.

The problem with psychology—it needs to be linear. It needs a trait or an event to have traveled from, and to be headed in some direction. But the most fascinat- ing elements inside of us are just like that crumbling

Parisian hotel—they are labyrinths—and inside the labyrinths are images that make little objective sense. I do not have a sister. And if I did, I would not want to see her debase herself. She could debase herself—but I would not want to see it. Or perhaps I would want to see it. But not to take part in it. Or perhaps I would want to take part in it. But only because to do so is forbidden. And the forbidden is no more than a change from what is not forbidden. Flower to flower, ashes to ashes, dust to dust.

4

I had another dream—a gargantuan dream that lasted
all morning—and I have now awakened in the midday,
adrift on the sea of time. I was lying in a field in the
basin of an ancient amphitheater. I knew it was ancient
because there were giant cypress trees inside of it.
A large crowd had piled in for some kind of celebra-
tion or festival. I had neighbors lounging and snoring
and socializing on all sides of me. My sister was back.
This time she leaned over me—I could smell her skin—
it smelled like her skin—that is, it smelled familiar, as
if I had known it for years in the bottomless logic of
dreams—she leaned over me and she planted an open
mouthed kiss on my lips, and together we breathed each
other's air in our shared darkness—then just as quickly
as she had materialized she disappeared somewhere up
in the wide bowl mezzanines of the structure—I could
just faintly spot her in the mottled crowd. The rest of
the dream I spent wandering among these countless

people, looking for her. I wandered so long that I got hungry, and I somehow collected a bag full of carrots and pretzels. I sat at a table in the amphitheater café staring at this meager meal while the main act trickled onstage—and a spotlight was trained on a pianist as he flipped his tails over the back of the ebony bench and began to spool forth a difficult piece with enviable mastery. I looked down at my bag of misshapen carrots, and I had the feeling that my sister was gravitating towards the pianist. I lost my appetite. I left the amphitheater and stepped out somehow into the streets of San Francisco. Everything was on an unnatural angle, and the light kept getting eclipsed by fog. I do not know how you ever say "everyone", but in this case, everyone was trying to get to the ocean. So I flowed along with this river of people. My brother—my actual brother—called to me and encouraged me to run faster. He was out in a field beyond a screen of (again) cypresses—I could not see him but I could hear his voice. Faster, he cried. Faster. So I ran faster. But no matter how fast I ran, there were people who overtook me. Some were cheating—they were flying. I ran out of energy, and had to stop to regain my breath. My brother was still calling for me to get back in the race.

"You can do it James!" he cried.

"I cannot do it, Daniel," I said.

"You can, yes, you can do it."

"No, Daniel I cannot."

"But you must, we must get to the water!"

"Daniel."

"What?"

"What are we doing here, Daniel?"

He did not have the chance to answer this question—I woke up and emerged into the sweltering half light of my bedroom. I made a pot of coffee—and I did not cry this time, at least not yet—it was only a few minutes ago. It is too hot to emerge, and there is nothing left living outside. If I am to collect, I must now do it inside of my mind. I only ever desired to *be* in the unknown—to walk in the cold and refreshing mist of ignorance and to see it congeal into a life form symbolizing beauty and innocence—only to disperse again the next moment, as I became aware that the path of discovery was all but endless. I did not dream that I would reach the end of my seeking, the end of my collecting, and that ecology would devolve into the gene sequencing of museum specimens in laboratories in Shanghai and Stockholm. What we thought are two species might now be seven—now we may all lop our ears off. Nature does not acknowledge or give two flying hoots about what we call its parts. This does not interbreed with that. So this vis-à-vis that is celibate and vice versa. But it may not be so, and it may not have been so, at some time other than this cursed

Anthropocene. And long after we have pulled the roof down on ourselves, the nameless wonders will abide and defy classification.

The terra incognita is inside me now, and my way will be no less arduous than the one that landed me here. I have written hundreds of scientific papers about the way plants and animals relate to one another. I have written not a single paper on the way a man relates to his dreams. Of all the activities we embrace, aside from our means of arrogating food and resources to ourselves, dreaming takes up the most space in our lives. If you count waking dreaming—the sensation of being removed from a moment and deposited in another—then with no contest we spend the majority of our lives roaming the unmapped architecture of our own minds. To what end?

Another vision followed the phantom lips of my nameless sister, the rumble and the piano chords of the amphitheater, the San Francisco fields, my dead brother. The vision was in a barracks in the far east—the landscape outside the windows was gently rolling hayfields interspersed with densely treed forests of pine and birch—alike to the forests of northern Russia. I know these forests, not from experience or study or film, but from my reading of *Anna Karenina* when I was seventeen. The forests were designed not so much for the proliferation of life—the winters are too harsh—but for the proliferation of light. Through the black background of the forest silhouette, and reflected up at you by the bed of scarlet pine needles, the sun reaches its peak of clarity. It is almost pure white. The shoe of Kitty swings over the back of a horse, and the laces of her shoe too are almost pure white. The most perfect shade is reserved for the whites of her eyes. She, too, a portrait of beauty and innocence.

The barracks is not unlike the one I live in now—both were once a secret from the world—but while my home was used merely to receive and redirect shipments of weapons and materiel, the one in my dream was used for the purpose of human extermination. The project was long over—and the remains of the fallen had been burned or buried. The gulag had been repurposed as a family camp of sorts. You had the sense, although you could not see it, that a lake was nearby, and that the lake, although wild and scenic, had been depleted for agriculture and desecrated with heavy metals from nearby mines. In the various huts and cabins of this family camp my entire extended family was deposited, and they went about their business of feasting and resting and engaging in passionate conversation about sleeping habits, aches and pains, college admissions, promotions, marriages, divorces, births, deaths, sportive pursuits, film recommendations, enemies, politicians, actresses, realtors, turncoats, generals, ship captains, neighborhoods, tax rates, islands, and automobiles. They discussed the provenance and the metaphorical characteristics of certain wines and fine scotches. They discussed the virtues, especially as one ages, of having a beer every now and then with breakfast. They discussed how they felt their feet and ankles started to swell, and they were more commonly subject to postural hypotension and fatigue. And in even more private circles they discussed the subject of marital alienation and even intramarital imbroglio. It seemed to me, surveying the gathering as I did from my dream perch, that the more simple a man was, the more content he was with his lot—akin to a goldfish in his bowl of infinite wonder—and I do not mean to say simple in a denigrating way—I mean to say simple as in calm, passive, unthinking, meditative. The expansive ones buckled and winced and groaned under the force of their thoughts—the sensation of imagination condensing as it hits the dry air of reality. They suffered from gout, rheumatism, migraines, bad hips, broken limbs, snapped sinews. They suffered from dizziness, agoraphobia, insomnia, joint disorders, sciatica, fibromyalgia, anemia, hypertension, hyperlipidemia, polycythemia, and constipation. They suffered too from addiction to the medications used to treat all of this—and so the physical world, in response to all this striving toward the metaphysical—got the visioning ones trapped in a vortex of self-defeat.

All this was evident to me with a moment's glance from my dream perch. In the next moment my family was gone, the gulag was operational again, and I was being slowly lowered into a barrel swarming with leeches and ticks. Aside from the underlying realization that this was just a dream, I did not regard my bleeding-out with fear, and I did not struggle against my captors. My feet were dipped into the water, and as I peered outside into the still pure white light I realized that death is nothing more than a beneficent rationing out of oneself to other bodies. By the time half my body was submerged in the water, and I began to feel the tugging of the leeches' teeth and the digging of the ticks' mandibles in my flesh and a concomitant weakness at the sudden loss of blood, I was entirely at peace with the exercise. How many times have I regarded a pinned butterfly, no less precious than me in the scheme of the universe, without feeling or regret, although I be the reason for its demise? So too will the open skies regard me, if they regard me at all.

5

—

I know who is with me on that bus—I had a continuation of the dream. Black hair, tiger-green eyes—it is *you*. How did I miss this essential detail, this keystone of my deepest self?

It has been rare, in my dreams, to feel the insides of another person. Maybe my dream-spirit is concerned that if I can have intercourse while asleep, I will never awaken—for the animal motivation will have been gutted from my waking life. How many naked bodies have I beheld in perfectly sculpted pink or fine olive glory—but not been permitted to touch? Last night, the force of my will—or it could have been *your* will—broke the back of the dream-spirit, and delivered you to me for hours. I knelt in front of you and took in your entire girlhood and navigated its architectures with my mouth by memory. You were standing, smoking a freshly rolled cigarette—and your voice, urging me onward, was as stylistically brilliant as it was the first time I heard it.

Your teeth were stained with wine. Your arm cradled a bronze sculpture of a missile. In such moments, we are reminded of a need we never knew we had. The need to feel our own mortality piece by piece—the need to not care in the least when it comes or how—this is the feeling I had when your tiger eyes met mine—like being hit by the concrete trucks of life and death all in one crossing. Why are Neruda and Borges so obsessed with the tiger—is it that you have lived many lives, in many forms, and in your multitude of journeys you have visited their beds as well?

Miller wrote *The Colossus of Maroussi* about a man named Katsimbalis. Katsimbalis was plagued by neuritis, vertigoes, pains between the ears, handicaps, lapses in vision, and addictions. He was always plagued and he was always pushing to discover more and to give more to the people around him and to indulge them in his explorations, his feats of daring, his nightlong narratives, his imaginative voice. He was adored. Katsimbalis never produced any art, Miller said, because he did not need to—the work of art was the man himself. Now imagine if Katsimbalis were a woman, and imagine that she did, from a young age, give the world gifts of her own genius, wrought by her hand in plaster, in steel, in clay, and in pigments. So I begin to describe you, your essential presence. You suffer more than Katsimbalis because you feel compelled to leave something for the keeping after you are gone.

I need to take a break. I *need* to take a drink. Nothing stands between me and the pain of having given away the world.

Let us go back to the beginning. Your fingers were black with charcoal and your nails were caked with other detritus of creation—paints, plaster of Paris, adhesives, nicotine. We did not speak directly to each other, out of respect for our mutual friend, and I did not see you again until the next fall.

I saw you early in the morning in the library stacks, you were carrying Rabelais. We met that night by pure inevitability—there were no words exchanged, no plans made. Your body had the scent and feeling of a miracle. The fulminations of so many eons and the tears of so many bereavements and the blue light of so many ecstatic dawns were enclosed in a pale miniature that I could have ported in the palm of my hand. Each evening we lay down on the roof of your tenement and we spotted the cold flame of Venus and the molten madness of Mars. The whole universe dissolved in the phosphorescent pool of your iris. The whole of mine and the whole of yours—they fell into orbits of each other's gravitation. I took you to my open-air laboratories—the forests of Wisconsin were then so rife with fauna that in order to demonstrate the myriad morphologies of winged life all one had to do was shine a light through a sheet and wait. You led me through the stacks in your many tongues and demonstrated that the history of the human mind was at least as rich as that of its environment. It is to you that I owe the furnishing of so many mirrored corridors in my being that would have remained cobwebbed and vacant.

Two confessions. The first is to you, the second is to the world. The first I will not air, because there is no good in going to one's grave knowing he will do harm to the one left behind, like the obverse of Orpheus. I take more pleasure in the second: It has been so natural to carry you with me that you have become featherweight—and so I must peel off the layers of my own skin to realize that they are yours, too. I never did leave you behind. No woman or girl who has ever made a wrong turn into my bed has ever been privy to the sanctum sanctorum of my soul. Not Sofia, not Cassandra, not Carlita, not the hazy queue of PhD candidates and postdocs and mendicants and supplicants in my tutelage, not the perfumed prostitutes, not the anemic Eastern Europeans, not Felicia or Alicia, not even the ones for whom my whole body ached down to the marrow. Not even the ones to whom I sacrificed years off the end of my life—years whose nonexistence stares me in the face like the blinding light of the beacon of the Stygian ferry—not even they could steal me from your blackened hands. With or without your knowledge, I have kept your glowing coal safe from all suitors.

We had to hide somewhere—the forces acting on our senses were, still are, either so elevated or so harrowing as to be unbearable. So we hid inside one another, and nobody found us.

6

——

I was on the highway, down in the tree tunnels near Cañas Dulces. It was raining in the way only rainforest nights can rain. A lodge loomed in many terraced stories of orange stucco and mirrored glass over the road—the Mariposa. In a rare ensemble my whole extended family was there in one room, the living and the dead, and we were all whispering to each other with tears welling in our eyes. Just then, out the window in moon silhouette, the pregnant cap of Rincón loomed and tumesced, and it blew off in a catharsis that blackened even the black sky. The Earth's bowels began to ooze out. Rivers were turned cadaver grey and overwhelmed villages. The rain came down as sulfurous bird droppings all over everything. At morning the dawn could not find a place to pierce the lagoon of darkness that hung above us. The day came and went without light. We took our headlamps up to the park and tried to survey the damage. The wreckage was entire—there was nothing left. We—it was vague who composed we—but I knew you were not there—made our way back to the Mariposa and contemplated our means of suicide.

This morning I awoke to the frantic pounding of my blood brother Ilario's fists on my bedroom door. In our decades of working together, through all the trials of our improbable projects, through all of our rustic and sometimes entirely deprived and desolate stints in every remote biological station in this country, the man has never roused me out of a sound sleep. Without the benefit of coffee he threw me into his truck and we drove down the Interamerican towards Cañas Dulces.

"Estalló! Estalló!"

"No. No credo."

"Explotó! Explotó!"

"No, no credo."

"Sí que puta estalló!"

"No credo."

We dropped off the Santa Rosa plateau and into the pasturelands and got a glimpse of the cordillera and the sky. I threw up between my legs. The top half of the mile-high massif of Volcan Rincón de la Vieja is gone. The slopes have been desecrated, raped by lava flows. The only difference from my dream is that every ripple of the mushroom cloud hanging over the volcano is illumined by the innocent light of the sun, and the sky is a fragile baby blue as if this is its first morning of awakening. I threw up between my legs again. I asked Ilario to stop the car. I threw up on the roadside. I threw up on the roadside again. I felt slightly better—better because there was nothing more I could do. Ilario too was beside himself, but his sanity was preserved by the degree to which mine was lost. He suggested we go up to Curabandé to see if there was anyone we could help. I could not think of a worse idea—to grovel in the shadow of the monster. He suggested we go out to Pocosol and meet with the park staff. I could not think of a worse idea—who knew who was dead or who was alive—we might have lost Eduardo, we might have lost Carolina. He suggested we go to Santa Rosa and at least show our faces. I demurred. We returned here, and I made coffee and we both smoked (and I continue to smoke) contiguous cigarettes. We worked the phones for a couple of hours, and it became clear that no one we knew personally had outright died. It was only the trees, the bugs, the birds, the mammals, the reptiles. San Cristobal is gone. San Gerardo is gone. La Perla is gone.

We got stoned and fell back asleep. I woke up in the high daylight and, seeing that Ilario had left, I got in my truck and drove down the Santa Rosa plateau towards Cañas Dulces again. I thought that maybe my senses had deceived me. Some clouds had settled along the brow of Rincón, beyond which one normally could not see—such that even on an uneventful day the top of the mountain could be missing, and we would not know. I drove up to Quebrada Grande and banged up the road to Cacao station—the road was so dry it took me no more than ten minutes from the soccer field. The soccer field.

"La vida es pensar de sus niños."

I banged up to the station, which was uninhabited or in the midst of a siesta—I could not tell and I did not want to know. Specimen bags were sparse. In this massive *veranillo* no one was finding anything—and if they did they might be saving its life by putting it in a bag with a handful of living leaves. There were no beans on the stove, nor was there a sense that beans had been recently on the stove. There were no towels or clothes on the line. Some small pairs of shoes were collected and perched at the edge of the concrete porch. The tap was running—a stream no larger than a drip was leaking out of it. No larger than a drip, and when I approached to turn it off, I found that the tap was all the way open. I stood watching the stream for what could have been an hour. Then I continued up the trail.

In the most compelling version of the story, I climbed to the scorched top of Cacao, looked across the valley at the blown off top of Rincón, finally threw myself off Cacao's razor ridge, and so spiraled to my death. This is how I have planned my death ever since I blazed the trail up Cacao and witnessed the evergreen, burgeoning black magic of its pygmy cloud forest: I tilt off the edge, and I die in suspension, just as gravity takes hold of me and flings me against the tree limbs and splits my skull and flays my guts and gouges out my eyes and breaks all my bones. I die in equilibrium with the earth that bore me up. I am broken apart and woven into a million forms, each with its own peculiar curiosity and quest.

I reached the top, and I glimpsed in one ken the Atlantic and the Caribbean, the rugged and irreducible wildness of my homeland scorched to cinders, and crowning it all the exploded skull of Rincón. I realized, there is nothing left for me here. There is not even death left for me here. The feeling was of a chill, a monstrous chill bordering on panic, as if someone had removed all my clothes and my skin, and my organs were out there jangling in the wind. I ran down the mountain. When I reached the truck my teeth were chattering and could have exploded each other apart. I raced down to the Interamerican. I came home. The only option seemed to be to write. Perhaps if I talk to myself in straight sentences, I will be able to find out what I will do—or who I am supposed to be. So, James Santo, what will you do, and who are you supposed to be?

7

This morning, I awoke in a depression deeper than the firmament. It took hold of my body like an anchor dragging at a ship. Every bone, every muscle, every drape of skin, even my ears and my eyes, are being pulled down. Every thought somehow is being pulled down too. My vision does not seem to want to focus. My shoulders feel like they were pasted to the sides of my head all night—they are the only part of me that will not fall, but then they do fall, and only with pain. With pain, and they spring up again. They spring up again, and I cannot put them down. Then I try to go outside, and the light blinds me. It blinds me and it drives outrageous icepicks through my eyes. I see the words in my mind clearly, but when they come out of my pencil they are removed from my vision, the page is always just behind reality. It would seem that this is where all the insight lies—just behind reality—but the theorists were mistaken—it is not a comfortable or an insightful place to be. It is not a sophisticated place to be. It is the mass grave of my dreams. It feels that the whole vision—my vision of being a savior to the world, has been sucked away, and now, without that vision, I lack the power to create another one. What is the world?

Those too lazy or too blind to work out the answer to this question claim there is no answer, and there can be no answers. I cannot conceive of a more craven way to approach the universe than to see it as the plaything of a child who hands his mother an imaginary bouquet of flowers. No truth! All is mediated! All is fabricated! Break it all down! We did—many times over—first the human world then everything outside the human—we broke it all down. The job is done, and the cretins are still talking. They will be talking until there are no bees to pollinate their food plants, and they will be living off Coca Cola and Bosco. *The universe is far more complex than your mind.* It is a symphony of relationships so elegant that only the most learned of us can even *hear* it, let alone begin to understand it. The music. I have been listening to the music made by the universe since my senses first awakened. I have lived not on food, not on money, but on the artistry of the divine force that makes the wings of an insect, makes the tendrils of an orchid, makes the ground to undulate and to cradle the rain. Each morning I have lived out the dream of getting closer to the center, closer to an understanding of how this divine force is constructed, and what moves it makes. It is no wonder that this morning I awaken in pain—my food source is gone. In my former life I had an insatiate desire, a bottomless want, to be where I now sit. Every day spent in the suburbs, every scheduled conversation with the director of this, with the curator of that, with the doctor, the therapist, the teacher, the colleague, every night pitched through with metallic noise and the wails of sirens, every realization that there was some task to do that would lead only to more tasks to do, every award ceremony, every speech, every sit down with the administration, every round table discussion, every tutorial, every lecture hall, every broken student, every flowerbed, every day spent fearing Sofia, every subway ride, every dinner party, every debate, every game of poker, every vacation by the seashore, every stolen evening at the flat of a mistress, every morning abysmally hungover and with botulism running in my veins, every need to explain why I could not do what was expected of me, every need to explain why I had done what was not expected—in short, every day and night spent in the built environment was a curse to me. I wanted nothing more—since I can remember—I wanted nothing more than to shed the leveling influence of society—the way it took any semblance of difference, of originality—such as my outsize ability to *love*—and decapitated it. It is not the fault of people. At least I do not fault them. What would faulting them do? I have no recourse. My mother and father, too, had no recourse. And their mother and father, and the mothers and fathers before them—no recourse. Even if I could have put Sofia in jail. Or if I could have painted a smile on her face. There would be another Sofia behind her. Marriage is the only legal institution in which one human's ownership of another human is still permitted. You can unbind yourself, but only for a time, while your instincts catch their breath. A moth will suicide itself against a streetlamp before it will forego a shot at the pheromones upwind. So too will the man.

I wanted nothing more than to get out of the known world. Escape to the source of life, away from other voices, into the inscrutable voices of the wild. And as the cloud forests evaporate and turn to dust, my scheme of self-disappearance disappears. I sit here at the center. The music has stopped—it is quiet. I am still. I am still.

In my dream last night, we were walking together over a domed landscape. Grasses bucked and whirled in a celestial wind. The light of the sun was half-dawn, half-dusk and heavy as incandescent powder in the air. You were younger than I ever knew you—you were a girl just becoming a woman.

"This," you said, "is my heaven."

You had on your face a thin and tight-lipped smile, a suggestion of amusement and a suggestion of something deeper—the edges of the lips were pressed inwards and downwards—a type of knowledge—written on your cheeks that were as taut as porcelain—a type of knowledge that an old shaman would possess, after traveling to the tents of his ancient forebears while the village was asleep—except his cheeks would have the consistency of dried fruit, and the scars of his people's sins would be branded into his brow.

There was an interlude I cannot remember. Then we moved indoors, and the scene became recognizably domestic—it was a bedroom we had shared in my dreams before. Or it was a bedroom I had shared with someone else in reality. Your parents stood in the doorway, they uttered some approving words—albeit not approving of what was about to happen—they more seemed to approve of my presence as guardian, as an overseer. We were left alone. I smelled my own fear as much as I smelled your prurience. I turned around—you were half naked on the bed—your bottom half—and in response to your entreaties I found myself trying to calculate, in a dream-stupor—the difference between our ages. You were refined, ripe, perfect, and I had already wasted away.

Before I could even reach out and touch you, you were gone—so far gone that I could find no trace of your impression or scent in the bedsheets—and a crowd outside was raising an uproar and demanding my capture and imprisonment. I had tried, in inexorable and miserable vanity, to turn back time.

I looked out the window and into the black eyes of the crowd. I started to search the room for a weapon. In my dream mind the relief of bloodletting, the release of pressure, the loss of discreteness, calmed me. Just as I happened upon a real steak knife that you had planted in the hand of a jackrabbit, the dream-spirit indulged in a bit of old school montage. We were transported to a bordello—you, me, and two women exactly resembling you, but for subtle differences in thigh thickness and the heights of their brows, and but for their age and profession—they were every bit of twenty-one, and they were professionals. The sheets now were not blue but white. You pushed me into their arachnid embrace, and you exited stage left.

This morning I awoke in a depression deeper than the firmament. It took hold of my body like an anchor dragging at a ship. Every bone, every muscle, every drape of skin, even my ears and my eyes, are being pulled down. . . . I lived a life of romantic desperation under cover of a man who was saving the world. Now that the world cannot be saved, my cover is blown. Is there anything more than the bond between lovers? Is there anything more than foreseeing that this bond, like a chemical bond between two units of reduction, will banish the toxic payload in one's life once and for all? Will jettison the unit of death that we were all born with—the dose of cyanide that hangs around our necks—and free us from having to port it around with us to every single engagement? We all have our ticket back to the underworld, and there is no missing the train, there is no apotheosis, there is no escape of the physical reality of here today, gone tomorrow. There is the decision to waste one's energy on an imagined form of a higher existence. There is the decision to pursue tokens of transcendence—the goods, the property, the titles, the men or women who mirror us, or whom we imagine mirror us—or to let them go, to live inside oneself—to disappear from view—to exist as a self-proven reality.

I am still heavy, but at this point I have brewed coffee, and I have a certain expectancy of the dawn. Strange, how so quickly one's tune can change. Whose hands are playing this piano?

I should report another one of the dreams I had last night. We—who were we?—we were in Harvard Yard, and stands were set up to view a famous lecturer. She was an esteemed colleague who claimed a special standing in Mathematics. She held up a deep blue wooden board with golden numbers engraved in it. Just before coming upon this scene, I had walked the parking lot looking for food scraps. I had found a sack of cookies, a handful of pound cake. I could not find milk to wash it down . . . it was a shame . . . She held up a matrix of numbers, and she asked the crowd to find a rule that predicted the relationships between the numbers. If there is no rule, we call this chaos, she said, but what if there is something between rule and chaos? The scene shifted to one of the many basements of the library, where the walls were indistinguishable from mirrors, and the voice in my head expressed dire uncertainty over whether or not the space really ended. Stacks upon stacks—a catacombs of thought. I reached the Life Sciences area by smell, and then fumbling blind through forests of unknown titles I found the shelves assigned to the memory of James Santo. His volumes were tight to one another, meaning he was not as picked over as one would have hoped. Did no one read James Santo anymore? What about *One Thousand Specimens Previously Unknown*? What about *Natural History of Amistad*? What about *On the Convenient Fictions of Evolution*, and *The Emergence of Life*? What about *Wars of Ants and Wars of Man*? What about my treatise on the future of conservation? What about the popular classics? The easy reads? Nothing? I sagged, and I sagged so deeply that I felt I was falling through the floor. If I did not escape the stacks soon, the concrete would suffocate me. I flew down innumerable staircases that narrowed as I descended. For some reason I stopped to pick my nose—a fatal mistake. I spilled out into the Yard, but

I was too late. Tsunami sirens were sounding, and, stylized in electric blue by a traditional Japanese cartoonist, the waves were ten stories high. Screaming, gasping, clawing for life, I was eclipsed.

The dream can be seen in two ways. I am certainly in terror of something—I am in terror—but for once it is not terror of Sofia—it is terror of an unknown. Disappearance—there is fear of disappearance in the dream—of irrelevance—and in this sense it is an *old* dream, because such fear defined my youth. I needed to consider myself at least an equal of the theorists, the thinkers I admired unconditionally—including my lady colleague who so elegantly posited a third order—one in which reason and its antithesis are in constant conversation, but one that does not depend on either for its existence. I needed the comfort of knowing that my students would inherit—if not my opinions and perspectives—at least my drive to find out a piece of what was unknown to me. The dream symbolized the miscarriage of all these desires. I can imagine that when a woman feels a dead fetus leaving her body, it is as if she is sinking in concrete, or drowning in the ocean.

But there is more to this dream than my depressed mind appreciated when I woke up in a gasping delirium, with my heart leaping out of my chest like a flushed hare and my whole body throbbing as if deep sound waves were being pulsed through it. There is more to it—not in an absolute sense—because who knows what there is to dreams anyway—but there is more to it in my resistance of my fate. I saw the waves rising up over the Harvard Yard and my heart screamed out not to be engulfed but to be saved. I have more to live, dear self. I have far more to live than I realize. I have a different kind of work to do, one I do not yet understand, but one that may compare in weight to everything I have done before. Or may compare in weightlessness. To hold weight. What do we mean? Do I hold weight? I feel that I hold less and less weight. James Santo is being chopped and scalloped. James Santo is a sort of legless being. Without his world and his women, James Santo is like a figure chiseled into the stone façade of a forgotten church. Yes—forgotten. To be erased from the collective consciousness, to be unknown—that is new to me—to be no one. Now I can breathe. My kingdom is starving, it is burning, aching, dying. Carcasses are being removed from the market square, the wells have all been poisoned, and vandals have raided all the sacred sites. My domain has shrunken to the size of my mere body. So—

8

I have filled six notebooks, and it seems I take some form of pleasure in this exercise. Looking back at the beginning—at my fragmented, agitated, even I dare say disenchanted prose—I feel that the practice of spilling some of my blood on the page each morning and night has released something in me. The art of phlebotomy is not lost—but one must bleed oneself on one's own—and do it not with razor or with anguish but with diligence—and then by removing all other outlets for whatever it is that one calls this.

Today I tried to drive down to Playa Blanca. I could not drive down to Playa Blanca because I was too weak, and my body was paralyzed. I made it only so far as Little Tibet, but I could not get out of the car. I could not get out of the car the same way a mother cannot look at the body of her child laying in a casket. In that way I cannot look at Little Tibet anymore, I do not want this to be my memory of a landscape that sustained me, that sustained tens of millions of nameless winged things that searched for one another by the reflection of the sun against the cold face of the moon, that adored Felicia and Alicia, that sheltered their dreams, that sheltered other dreams that have since died before finding a body to inhabit. So I did not get out of the car. On the drive back from Little Tibet, my vision started to blur, and my hands and feet shook, I could barely grip the wheel. When I got out of the truck, I walked like a catatonic into my cabin, which appeared so utterly broken down that it was almost unfathomable that anyone had inhabited it. My home, no more than an outhouse at the brink of the vanquished unknown. I lay down on the floor and the whole world faded away. I could breathe, but the air was not pervading my body, it was just shuffling back and forth. I waited. The shaking and the emptiness did not stop for about an hour, at which point I was a lost husk, a brittle shell of a human. My heart was dancing a vaudeville routine in my chest. I breathed my bland meager air one way and the other, I forgot about my existence, and I drifted off to a dream riddled midday sleep. Now I am awake and it is dark, and I have never yearned so badly for one day to bleed into the next, to release me into the next stage of my existence, for better or worse it does not matter. To forget—to forget—if it would rain, I believe that the rain would not even need to touch me, it would only need to touch my senses, its neverending treatise on delicacy would only need to whisper its repetitions into my body and it would wash away those things I have forgotten how to forget. For a time it would wash them away, and give me a chance to refill the well at the center of all this with something pure—or to believe that I could be purified. The idea that the god of six billion would bother to reach down to purify one old, bloated, hoary and sinful man would be too much to ask. But I need to believe that there is something benevolent behind the gallows. Something benevolent and extraordinary. A life force that will penetrate the drab outer curtain of my being. It would happen sometimes during a particularly cathartic storm when I was out in the forest and the humidity was being cut by the rain and the air was thinning out and the trees were coming alive in the breeze. I would feel something not unlike an electric shock in my chest that reverberated into my gut and warmed the space where my legs met my torso—it would be a monstrous insult to the feeling to call it merely sexual—what happened is that the elements brought me to life. I was translated from Santo on paper, with his egoes and his proclamations and his positions and his other falsities, to Santo in the flesh, who has no scrutable description—who is far more complex and far more all reaching and far more nebulous than a man. He is so far removed from all that is spoken by the rational mind and all that is sutured by force into the smooth face of the spirit and what is bled into our days by memory and what is tongue tied with the devil through the conscience and its upbraidings . . . he is so far removed from these things that he is beyond memory and forgetting. The things that held him by each sinew of his body, that tied him to a chair, that pulled him down towards the grave, are all gone and never existed. Santo in the rain—better yet just after the rain, when everything is silent and poised to multiply—he is the medium of a benevolence, that medium is all he aspires to be, and so he is entirely at peace with life and death—indeed the difference is meaningless to him, and he can fade into the sky or the ground just as easily as he can take a pull from his flask of water and be given perhaps another moment.

Whereas this fallow, this desiccated silence is the silence of awaiting something even worse than death to happen—the witnessing of annihilation, and knowing that I will be preserved as a vessel of all that was before—I will carry the rife, the pathologically inspired, the inundated, the lovestruck, the ageless, the inviolate former world inside of me—yes I will carry the rains—I will carry the rains.

9

My father was a classical systematist. He had an obsession with knowing things, and he seemed to know all things that could be gleaned from written material, from today's newspaper back to the imaginary prehistories of the sacred texts. He also had a keen sense of who did and who did not know as much as he did, and when your face rested in uncertain formation in response to one of his references, say, "*Charles Mingus was the unsung Art Blakely of the jazz piano*", he would jack up his gaze and fix you in mute astonishment until you admitted utter ignorance. Last night I saw that strigine face in a Rococo seminar room in the clouds. My father was dressed in a three-piece suit, and the chain of a pocket watch snaked across the taut belly of the vest. The ensemble had been etched by chalk lines as heavy as the vapor trails of falling stars. There was chalk on his fingers and chalk on his face where he had pulled at his moustache and chalk on his head where he had brushed back his uncommonly long hair from his eyes. He had the crisp but heavy smell of Marlboros on his breath, and there was something sinister underneath them—Cutty Sark or a type of Seagram's. On the blackboards behind him were drawn phylogenetic trees comprising the descent of *Astraptes fulgerator,* a small flashy skipper butterfly, on the one hand, and Homo sapiens, an antlike and wasp-like organizer of colonies and hives and murders, on the other hand. The trees looked very different: for one the *Lepidoptera* tree was the size of a Volkswagen bus, and the human tree was the size of a postcard.

"What do you take from this?" my father asked.

"What do you mean, take from it?" I said.

"What do you take from it!" he cried, and he smashed a piece of chalk down on the seminar table so hard that it vaporized.

"There is nothing to take from it, it is simply one diagram of our ancestry. You could draw so many diagrams, with so many shapes and sizes. I could draw one of us, reaching back a billion years. Here, give me the chalk."

"What a god damn cop out! You will not take the chalk, you will not draw a thing! You will tell me what you take from this. This is the story, whether you like it or not! Assume—assume! That this is the story, now tell me what it means."

"You go out in the forest, Father, you go out and you look, you observe, you wait, you search, you find, you listen. You listen. Do you hear a story being told? Do you hear a narrative? Is there something linear, branching, elegant happening? Or are there circles—days and nights, dry and wet, longer and shorter—that throw off slightly different results like wheels throwing off sparks? I go out in the forest, I hear repetition. I hear the birdsongs, I hear the bugs' calls, I hear the breezes, I hear the rain. I hear the unbelievable silence of the sunrise. This is not linear at all, it is not progression, it is experimentation, it is improvisation."

"You're a nihilist then. My son, a nihilist! You cannot avoid the facts, son. You cannot avoid the facts!"

"What facts do you mean, Papa?"

"You are giving up on this." He almost soundlessly pressed a fresh piece of chalk against the phylogeny of the skipper. "Which is your prerogative. But you cannot give up on this." He pressed the chalk with delicate authority against the postcard sized ancestry of us. "They have had 200 million years to make a go of it. I do not mean to be callous, but they had their time in the sun, James. We, we are just beginning."

"Our happiness . . . my happiness. It depends on them." I stiffly indicated the skipper. "So we must be a part of the same tree."

"Oh my god," he whispered, and he paced in front of the blackboard and the nebulous scene outside. It got slightly darker in the room, as if the sun was setting somewhere. Then it got violently lighter, as when the clouds part after a rain. "Are you going to listen to the lesson, kid?"

"I was just saying . . . "

"You were just saying. But I've been here, kid. I've been exactly where you are. I've been here a million times before. And you will not . . . " He hiked up one leg of his suit and propped a heavy black boot on the table. For some reason he was wearing red socks with miniature Christmas trees printed on them. "You will not . . . "

"I will not."

"You will not . . . "

"I will not."

"You will not listen to the lesson I am about to tell you."

"What lesson is that?"

"It doesn't matter, because you will not listen."

"I am listening now, please pronounce it so that I can get this nightmare over with."

"You are too full of ideas, you always were too full of ideas. I could say it, but I do not even think you would hear me."

"I am hearing you now. Please, before I wake up."

"James, James! You should have heard me by now. I don't want to waste my precious energy on this if you will not listen!"

"Listening and hearing, I am doing both. Now please. Before . . . . What is happening to the room?"

"Over there? It's a storm against your unreality, James. I told you—I told you this would come and that you would need to be ready. Do you remember?"

"I do remember that, but now what? Now what?"

"I told you that your dreams would be compromised, that they would dissolve in the acid of the present day, and that you would need to remember one thing above all else. One thing!"

The walls of the building were being translated into the landscape. Spindly spruces with their arms full of virgin fluff. The sky was choked with white dust and prismatic white smoke. We were children. My father was pulling me and my brother Daniel in a sled. He had his arm around a fur-cloaked version of my mother, whose young smile made me burst into tears that streamed down my shirtfront and my pant legs and pooled in my shoes. I reached down to empty my shoes before they froze, and poof, I awoke in Santa Elena, the tears had dried and crusted my eyes shut, a shaft of midday light harbored a carousel of weight-less texture, and I was shaking again, my limbs seemed to have a phantom life of their own. A haze not unlike the snowstorm in my dream enclosed me as I tried to pack my things. There were too many things—I left them—all but these notebooks and a thrashed-together suitcase full of dirty clothes. I cranked my old Land Cruiser down the Interamerican as fast as she would travel to the airport thronged with tourists carrying farm-raised *Morphos* encased in glass like prisoners of war—and throwing the keys to an astonished *taxista* I abandoned her in the parking lot.

10

——

I am still on this plane. The whole place is asleep and I am the only one waking, even the babies and the hobbled old nuns are asleep. Even the fat stewardesses are asleep. Even the boisterous exchange students are asleep. I am like a moth in a sea of butterflies.

The flight arrives at Charles de Gaulle in what appears to be seven hours. I have had enough of the hours. I want to get lost in time. And I hate foreseeing, or getting tangled in the exercise of thinking that one is foreseeing, something that is guaranteed to be different from the image I have in my mind. The soothsayer is constantly beset with incomprehensible surprise. For example—how did Sofia, who hates Costa Rica more than any other place, who professes the consummate inability to stand the heat, who would rather eat human excrement than let a beetle crawl up her wrist, end up nonetheless in Costa Rica, and on a day when the affair with my assistants had reached its dovecote apogee and showed no signs of retrograde blackbird tragedy? How did Alicia, the angel, the most virginal, the snow white dryad of the pair, the symbol of all that was sacred—the protectress of my aspirational heart—the quiet one, the delicate one—how did she find herself thrust entirely out of her skin—how did she end up transmogrified, picked apart, offered up—rendered into a negative of herself—we will never know. Felicia, who was more hardened against the winds of fortune, who was the catalyst for all this glory and bloodshed—who was our warrior monk, our dark priestess—she too was broken.

The rains had kept me up all night. When the first songs of the waking birds emerged, I made coffee and took it to the truck and went for a drive. The land was still lush, soggy, resplendent, overflowing with life. Mist hung in the treetops. The sunrise emerged like the advent of a new universe. The sky threw off its cloaks and flashed improbable and endless. The howlers rolled out their calls like waves of giant boulders. Too tired to know where I was going, I let the truck drive me. It took me up through Quebrada Grande, but instead of taking the turn to Cacao, it continued towards Dos Rios, into the darkness of Rincón's northern shoulder. A teleologic sort of negative pressure was drawing us to San Gerardo.

I do not know if the flight is long enough for me to describe that lost landscape. Imagine if the entirety of Saint Peter's Basilica were hidden on a side street in a tiny Umbrian village, and only ten or twelve people knew about it. I climbed into the heights of the nave. I kissed the rose window. I looked out from the papal balcony. I whispered my prayers to the deity whose hand wove these mysteries. Elated, exhausted, I returned home.

There was an alien truck in the driveway, very expensive, a city truck, a truck of the haute bourgeoisie. Alicia lay in the dirt outside the shack. Her bedclothes were wrapped around her in a Rococo caricature of classical suffering, her cheek was bruised and her face was soaked through with different sorts of tears and her eyes bulged from her forehead like pearlescent sores. I took her into my arms. She was shivering, shivering, shivering like a small animal dying of shock and exposure. She could barely breathe. I could feel her pulse all over her body, it was as if her limits were being redrawn with each heartbeat.

"She is inside, James, that monster. That monster you call your wife."

I experienced what can only be described as reverse metamorphosis—I was changed from a winged messenger of the gods into a larva.

Out of Alicia's mouth came the unspeakable. It was miles—it would take me miles of ink to record her lament—and it would take me just as many miles to record the montage that swept through my mind as I enclosed her and tried to stem her sadness. When I try to write her words, my hand starts to shake and lightning pains crop up in my skull and my teeth assemble to destroy one other and a gordian knot forms in my stomach and I want to tear open a hole in this airplane and spiral down at maximum speed, I want to nosedive into oblivion.

What happened next, I only set down for the purpose of forgetting.

A haggard Sofia and a bloodstained Felicia walked out of the shack, *arm in arm*. What could have united them? I do not want to know what could have united them. I have so many misdeeds that to unearth them would be to commence an entire generation of penance. There is no time!

Married, Heaven and Hell passed by me and Alicia as if we did not exist and they entered the rapacious automobile and drove away. I was alone with the hollow frame of Alicia in the boiling air of the afternoon.

We went inside and I bathed her and put her to bed. I tried to make love to her, but she was stiff. I tried to speak to her, but she was mute. I made fried plantains and eggs for her, but she would not eat. I made her tea, but she would not drink. After four days of this, she started to show signs of dehydration and anemia. Her fingers were wrinkled as if she had spent too long in a bath. When I pulled down her lower eyelids, they were nearly as pale as the eyes they couched. The skin started to adhere to her hands and feet and to become diaphanous. Her hair began to fall out. I tried throwing her in a cold shower, but she just stood there mute, impervious, her head hanging down and her spine protruding like a dorsal fin. Then she started going for the knives—not to attack me, but to attack herself—and I scooped her up in a blanket—she weighed little more than a hundred pounds—and walked her onto a plane bound for Boston, with strict instructions that she check herself into to Mass General.

Now happily Alicia is laid out among the haunted and the screaming, she is hooked up to a digital octopus that is showering her with a cascade of irrelevance— that she is within acceptable limits and fit for life as a human being. Or like me she has found fortitude but lost faith in everything again and is on a plane back down south, where she will found a colony of lotus eaters and swear off sanity forever. I should have told her I am not really a *man*, I am a force that transforms everything in its path—bugs are found frozen stiff and impaled on the boards—ideas are found to be condensed into articles and books and unraveled into dust—women and girls are found in equal parts immortal and forlorn. I am not really a man—I am a channel through which energy flows at different momentums, forming eddies and whirls and rapids and black holes—and I lead out to the sea, which is serenity on the surface, but otherwise is chaos and blindness. I am a vessel for idiosyncratic magnetism. My loves are like the spirals of a galaxy— they sweep up the heady and glowing planets, the dead moons, and the space flotsam all in one embrace—and they are weightless but fixed in alienation from one another—fixed from an explanation as to why—and fixed in a teleology whose shimmering end is always withdrawing itself behind a curtain of black.

11

Forgotten—forgotten. It is dizzying this weightlessness, this feeling of dropping the sandbags of the past
and floating up into the blue mist. Perhaps the grand-
est luxury of living in Paris is to be unknown—the
oblivious and unhailing faces of the strangers on the
streets. I am no longer a curiosity, a carnival freak,
my name is no longer currency in any conversation.
My opinions have no shine, no spit, no polish to them,
and my thoughts are no longer poisoned by fame.
I have no further need to thread the needle of natural history with a theoretical thrust. It is clear to me
that the world does not know rules, it does not know
frameworks—it has a life and a mind all its own—far
away from our debates. There is no argument happening when a moth approaches a leaf to lay her eggs—it
is doing what a man does when he sees the legs of a
woman wide open and hears her voice beckoning him
in—and there is no argument happening when that

moth is eaten by a bird. There is no dialogue between nature and anti-nature. There are no higher or lower impulses. There are no mistakes and there is no perfection. What mysteries our universal mother keeps, she buries in unexplored and impenetrable places, where the wheel of time turns in concentric circles. To riddle her with maxims, to ply her with quantities, to reduce her and tinker with her in the lab, to cull her trees and trap and count her messengers, to record her outward movements—all this is for naught—mere investigation will never reach the heart of our existence. That task is reserved for the exercise of openness to the unseen and unheard, to that which is not objective at all but singular, fanciful, rhythmic, inscrutable, and rooted in our own deep human past, the one we lived as spirits rambling the universe untethered and divine.

Speaking of untethered, I paid my attorney half a million dollars never to hear the name of S____ again— and so I shall not write it. I saw my things cut in half, and I signed over the deed to our Cambridge home, none of which produced any sort of reaction in me—my divestment fell on a deaf inner ear. I did not even realize I had such amounts in such accounts—I had no use for any of it. I live in a small apartment on Rue Saint Séverin— and the spaces here are in such miniature that one is both hidden from all others and blended with them—I feel that I am bleeding across my boundaries and into

those of pianists, barkeeps, teenagers, waitresses, dow-
agers, gentlemen, sculptors, priests, and booksellers. My
sanctuary—where I feel most safe, where my senses
feel most boisterous and alive—is the antithesis of what
it was before—the pendulum has swung on a half-cen-
tury period—I am a student, a very green student, of
humanity. Not of their wars, their politics, their great
figures, but of their eyes, their movements, their habits, their abstract and hidden intentions. These defy
description, they are felt, they are registered in the gut,
in the spine, in the reproductive organs, in the coccyx,
in the rectum, along the inner surface of the skull. They
are communicated in codes that we will never trans-
late because they are always shifting, and each individual, each author, each messenger uses a different code.
Each sees desire differently—in a different intensity, in
perhaps a different color, and hears it in a different key
and timbre. Try to fit our endless human matrix with a
rule, a line, an average—as we have done, to our incon-
ceivable peril—and you miss everything but the garbage
man in orange overalls, his mouth full of tobacco chaff,
his jacket besmirched with chicken grease and human
waste, his body a rusted wheel of addiction, his mind a
blank screen on which the statistically-predetermined
platitudes and meaningless matches of the world-incin-
erator are projected. You catch something indeed with
that best-fit line, but you miss just about everything

that is worth thinking about. Science—it was a game of best-fit lines, of averages, of statistical significances. I spent my life chasing the tree, the bat, the bird, the moth equivalent of a garbage man. I was the swarm of black flies over his head, waiting to see if he dropped any clues on the origins of life. I was his poor wife, watching him for signs of brilliance. I was the idealizer of his prominent breasts, his balding pate, his uncircumcised sex. I was the court painter of his expressionless face. I was.

The days are getting shorter and foggier, and the nights are turning into entire coliseums of experience. The back streets and their colors and their temperatures, their microclimates, their sounds and scents, are like a wilderness—and the Seine is the Amazon, the Congo, the Nile of this landscape. The Tour Eiffel is a very old ceiba tree. Montmartre is a volcanic promontory. Everywhere in this city—on the islands, in the squares, at the zeniths—there are monuments to the unspoken, the indescribable. The silence that is observed within these monuments is symbolic of the fact that the divine cannot be expressed in words. Out in the street the torturous plane trees grip the air in silence. The sound of one's feet against the beige stones of the Tuileries is a form of silence. The great rippling desert of the river flows in a gelatinous silence. The issuance from the fingers of the pianist in the jazz cave beneath the streets is not so much noise as it is a description of the movements of the smoke of his cigarette, or it is the actual thing that charms the smoke into the air. The cities of my past were places into which I needed to be pressurized. Everywhere there was irritant, there was superfluous *bruit*, there was fuckery and misfortune, and there was the cold and inhuman ignorance of the self-blessed, encased in their pinstripes and sheltered in their motorcars. Here it is different, the only pressure I feel is pulling me *in*, it is gliding me along the streets, and it is relieving me of any effort in my movements. At times I feel that volition has left my body—and I have a moment of terror, like awakening from a sound sleep on the back of a running horse—then I catch myself, and I am motionless among the movement of the city, I am like a dragonfly riding the current of a stream. One rainy reflection of a streetlamp off the cobblestone of an empty street can cause me entire days and nights of surplus sensation. What is there? What is behind all this? There is a force inside of me that no accounting can tally up. Or the force is in my surroundings, and I am just a conduit that has been closed for so many years that my opening is a flood of unexposed images—underground dreams. The output is a joy that feels like the most strident form of sadness—as if the two poles of the Earth were to meet like a person's hands intertwined behind their back. One could weep from expressionlessness, from the inability to craft from any mined material the bell that, once rung, would echo one's thoughts. The cry of a child who has no words at all—mixed with the laugh of a mystic who has exhausted all philosophy—mixed with one's inability to tell the difference.

12

I have taken up the piano. All form, substance, and language is subsumed in my movements. My fingers become a choir of voices, splicing time, space and sound into one theme, one melody, one taste. I play for nights at a time, with only enough intermission to have a smoke and a shower and to cook myself a simple meal as the fog rolls in and the sun sets again. I play with the house bands, the hustlers, the incognitos, the eternal faithful. We go four or five sets of everything, of hot swing, of acid jazz, of bossa nova, of heady bop, and of blues, through Parker and Monk, through Gillespie, through Davis and Coltrane and Hancock and Corea and Jobim, and we feather off into the rambling nameless of our own nascent compositions. I have started to appreciate, if not to sanctify, the quality of a wine drunk as it lends itself to mildness and endurance but is nonetheless transporting, as opposed to the manic spike and toxic letdown of liquor, or the bottomless blandness of beer. The bartenders serve us out of three-liter jeroboams, it tastes like the sweat of the soil. We drink, we forget all thought, we forget the forgetting itself, and the threading happens with the eyes riding the divide between inward and outward—I listen but not with intent—I play but not with premeditation—I have faith but not foresight—I have momentum but not force—I imitate the sound that forms inside of me but I do not copy it, lest the press of my pencil cause the line to disappear. When I do open my eyes to the material-ity of the instrument, when I do start to witness the shouts, the laughter, the parade of fingers, the slam of sticks, the gleam of cheeks, the trajectories of feet, the weight of the sweat-spangled brass, and when I realize that my own movements are a split-second prophecy of the unfolding of all others, the reality of the scene is too unlikely to comprehend, and I must close my eyes again until the music is distilled into the sacred silence of the basement after everyone has gone home. I take one last pull from my wine glass and close the keyboard on my piano, leaving it to curl up and sleep in its mahogany cradle. Tonight I came straight home—I ignored the bartender and the last lady straggler, whom I have already known and do not care to know any more. Outside my window it is the darkest part of night—the only movement is the cathedral stretch-ing its arms at the moon. The buildings are overcome with sleep, they rest their heads on one another in exhausted contentment. When I arrived home from the club I poured a coffee, and I listened to a record, then another. Then another. I laid down on the ground and I reached my arms and legs out until it seemed I was many meters long. I could almost touch the two sides of my study with my extremities. Then I got up and I approached my notebook. All the bodily energy is out of me, it has cascaded down my legs leaving just a small tingle of magnetism where my soles meet the wood floor. In the background the radiators are sighing, my ears are ringing icily from the music and the booze and the exertion. The reality of me is slipping, but I embrace the fact that my body is becoming immaterial. I have flashes behind my eyes of a phantom daylight. Single thoughts come and sweep me away for weeks, and deposit me back in my corner. Snow is falling heavily now, it swarms in a medium of extreme silence. As I write I receive telegrams from other lives. The landscapes, the architectures, the textures and tastes of those possible existences are so well known to me that each sensation is hyperreal—the feel of unnamed lips and embraces, the scents of bodies, and the inner cry from a place of untranslatable desire that will never be fulfilled. I scratch away with this charcoal claw at human history. Will it ever end? Has it yet begun? Along the Seine three girls chant Baudelaire's poem to the Creole through unpainted mouths. A house on the Quai whose shape is of a chevron takes the moonlight with averted eyes. The Dutchman is just stepping out of George's. His smile shatters his bearded, beery face. In a corner of Sainte-Clotilde, a prayer is found hovering in the form of a dancing flame with no candle. A girl creeps up on the prayer, she cups it in her hands and she slurps it into her belly. Outside, a freezing vagabond gets on the bus at the National Assembly, he rides all the way to the outskirts of Clichy, and among the human and architectural wastes, where ideas go to die, he bends down and makes himself a cocktail of the river. In the grey dawn of the apartment blocks he approaches each riparian sycamore in turn and kisses the bark and moves from tree to tree. From behind a wall of glass in the Place Dauphine, the man sheds incomprehensible tears—he is so drunk that he is sober again, and the days will not cease giving into one another—he must do something to get in the way of all this repetition.

In my dreams, the shoulders of Rincón are taking on the light of dawn in the same manner as the chevron shaped house on the Quai—but it starts to smolder and smoke and bleed, and its leafy headdress becomes a charred massacre. I walk the lower banks of the Seine, I recall walking the fields of Horizontes, and I think, this is a symbol, and my body is full of a warm, shivering sense of timelessness, and I do not know or care what the symbol purports to represent. What matters is the depth, not the substance, of the representation. What matters is the source of the message the world is trying to convey to me—the age of the parchment it is written on—I do not mind that the message is "MOURIR" or "VIVRE." When I was young I used to take the words themselves far too seriously—like a fortune teller reading the lines on the palm of the deity. The deity is the embodiment of destiny—the lines in his skin are relics of eternity—and there is no way to tell his past from his future. Eternity extends in all directions.

I can see the sky through a gap in the roofs facing me, and the dawn is starting to add blue to black, and white to blue, shade by shade every time I glance away from this notebook. Its veil lifted, the Rue Saint Séverin starts to chatter—pigeons, pensioners. I wait, and the street stretches its arms into the city. The last of the drinkers. The first of the book hawkers. Schoolchildren. A flock of runners. Tourists. A priest. The hungover ghosts of Hemingway and of Joyce, the bloodied ghosts of Robespierre and Marat, and the flabby naked ghost of Franklin. After and among those ghosts and indistinguishable from them are millions of nameless ones, still searching for their identities. They try on costumes—costumes of Franklin and Marat, of Robespierre and Joyce, of the flabby and naked Hemingway, of priests, tourists, schoolchildren, booksellers, and drunks. The city in turn stretches its legs into the street. The voice of an ambulance lodges its complaint against the indiscriminate sickle of the hereafter. Church bells punch out their retort—their heavy tone reaches through my window glass and vibrates everything—vibrates my skull, the record player, the bookshelves, the floorboards, and vibrates the etched lines of my past.

I looked you up as soon as I came to Paris. A few days passed of dizziness and stomach aches—I could not bring myself to call. I stared at the phone—at that time I was staying at a hotel off the Champs Élysées—and the phone, without saying anything, upbraided me for my cowardice. The streets too were having none of it. And the weather was bad, which made Paris look like an overembellished graveyard. I looked you up, and I did call. I left one message—I left six messages—I left twenty messages. You still have not answered. You may never. Maybe I do not want you to answer. I went by your apartment—it is in the Trocadero, in a neighborhood that is so elegant that it begs for destruction and rebirth—I went by your apartment, but I could not bring myself to ring.

Through music, through communal ecstasy—through a nightly routine of shedding all the indicia of bereavement—I am attempting to convince myself that it does not matter.

13

—

I woke up early in the afternoon, and I took an aim-
less walk in the city. The sun had already melted the
snow but for the icy footprints of men and birds who
had made it outside early enough to leave behind their
own personal fossils. The booksellers had dug out, runners loped through puddles and scattered the blue sky
into fragments. Hawkers and jugglers and mimes in the
Tuileries. The sidewalk narrowed as I passed the Opera
house and climbed la Rue Blanche towards Montmartre,
and I stopped in a nameless café for a coffee and a termite mound of coconut shards. The streets narrowed
so that one felt indoors, and the air was conditioned by
the scents and vapors of the people. The more crowded
it became, the calmer I began to feel. When I had been
out in the open, not a moment ago, in the Place de la
Revolution or in the overbroad Avenue de l'Opera, I felt
a savage wind blow through my body, the arctic chill of
uniqueness, of originality—the climate of genius—that

blows through a hole in the atmosphere straight from the nameless abroad of outer space—the air that tells us we must be something or someone before death wipes us from existence like a ball of lint flicked from the fingernail of the deity. But away from all that, up in the tight spaces, making one's way out of the plains of Paris and into the scrappy keep of Sacre Coeur, I felt a warmer shiver enter me—the reminder that I am no one and have no need of ever becoming somebody, that my memory is going to be lost among the names and dates that swarm the streets and line the cemeteries from here to Saint Denis, and beyond, and beyond. The people and their movements reminded me of the leaves in my forests—far back in the forests of my early days in Santa Rosa, when life was so dense and so close-cropped to itself that as you walked you continuously pulled back curtains on stages whose mysteries had never known human sight nor touch nor molestation. As the road became steeper, I noticed that even the eyes of the people coming at me began to resemble the eyes of the trees—skyward, and steady—or inward, dreamwrapt, enthralled by their own reaction to existence. I reached the Basilica. I dropped a few coins into the slot and lit two candles. Then I burst out into the open again before I could say a prayer.

The Rue Norvins and the Place du Tertre had the ceramic glow of a stage set—I had to get back down, quickly. I stopped in the Boulevard de Clichy for a quick wine and a bite by the sidebar, and I was seized by the sound of your voice in my mind, I was seized by the purity and the lightness, the cloudlike softness of your voice. I was turned to stone, crushed, pulverized, blown away by the sight of your eyes that shone kaleidoscopic and iridescent from within the sunless depths of my mind. I spent an agonizing few minutes waiting outside a phone booth for a man to finish a meandering story about a hunter and a giraffe. I dug in my pocket for a coin—I dialed your number—nothing. I dialed again—nothing. My hands started to tingle and my legs to buckle. I went in for another drink. My face took on a mask of pain, and as I opened my mouth to take a swig of wine, a lance shot out from behind my eyes and murdered my consciousness. I soldiered on—another drink. When I got out on the street the inside surface of my skull was frescoed with agony. I soldiered on—stepped into the blood red phone booth to call you again—fell to my knees.

In this my moment of humiliation before the godhead in the form of a deaf-mute telephone, I was completely out of coins. I had an image of you in the perfection of your youth. Your tears pooled in the palm that cradled your face. My body went numb, and it felt that I was being turned upside down and emptied of all my emotional contents—out onto the floor of the phone booth clattered invisible seeds buried before my mother was born—seeds buried before even the mother Earth was born.

I got up, I walked out of the phone booth, but shaken, and shaking. I followed the boulevard to and fro. I walked, but I was not sure how, the system had developed a glitch. The lights of the boulevard clouded my sight. I was many times my weight. The act of breathing, never a thought to me before, felt herculean. Waves—not waves of air but waves of some other substance—washed through me in a rhythm dislocated from the breathing—like two violinists wrangling for control of the conductor. Yet I walked down the boulevard, and I returned, probably a hundred times. Or was it six times, or nine? I did not know what would happen if I stopped—perhaps the music would stop too. Each time I visited the image of your face, I went into a floating paralysis—part of me collapsed and shattered in the street—the other part went on living. I vomited, I cried. My face was turned into a cubist wreckage. Yet the image of you would not cease to appear.

I didn't stop walking until something outside of myself gathered up my attentions. A pair of sandals, anomalous on a winter's night. Two sets of toes upon two sets of feet. The "ring-toes" were as long as the "middle toes". The pinky toes were curled under, so that your feet seemed to be signaling emphatically the number eight, and the visible members were fanned as if to adumbrate all the possible paths your feet could have travelled in that moment. I looked up. You peered at me through your eyes impossibly translucent even in the street's half dark, and your polished echelon of teeth was hidden behind a sphynx's tight-lipped smile.

"You have not aged a day, not a single unit of time since I last saw you on the streets of Monteverde so many thousands of nights ago," I said.

"You have," you said. "And you must have gone blind too."

"Can we ... "

I looked at you, but my eyes filled with tears and I could not see you.

"We cannot, James. We cannot. You can walk with me as far as the Opera and then I will go ... to meet ... we can go as far as the Opera."

"And then I will go no further ..."

"Do not make it this way, James. It is futile."

"I cannot ... how can you ... what is it I did—or did not do? ... I will give you anything—I will give you my life—what I have left of it."

"I would not know what to do with your life, James. I have a life of my own, I do not need yours. And please do not cry anymore or I will push you into the street."

I cannot simulate with words the beauty of your smile—how the words—no matter how harsh—felt like the vibration of the leaves in the gardens of paradise at the advent of the first spring.

"I will walk, I am walking," was all I could say.

"How is S____?"

"Do not speak that dread name."

"Why, you finally got away?"

"I did, I am alone."

"And the bugs?"

"The bugs are all dead. All but some stragglers in a place I call Little Tibet. Perhaps they will preserve the ways of their forbears, so that someone, someday, will study the greatest wonders of the world again. Or perhaps they are dead too."

"How about your children?"

"They are grown, they are alive."

"And yet you remain."

"What remains of me, I have been saving up for you."

"James, you cannot say that."

"I am not saying it, it is true."

We arrived at the Place Diaghilev, over which there lords in Baroque fury the Palais Garnier. I tried to take your hand—you ripped it away.

"James, this is the end."

You walked away from me—and I bottled up my pain and corked it so tightly that by the time I thought to light my next cigarette I was back on the Boulevard de Clichy. There you were again, but in a reinvented set of shapes—your feet had shrunken and tanned—your face had narrowed and darkened. Your pressed linen dress tied high on the waist had split in two and taken on a new texture—the neck had deepened and the hem had shortened to the crest of the pelvis.

I paid this new you and your withdrawn but well sculpted business partner or coeval to become a modern representation of Caligula's handmaids for the rest of the night. As I write this, the older one is whispering to the younger one (they are only separated by weeks from eighteen and each other) that my entire apartment now smells like lilac. It would have been impossible for the Romans not to have enslaved for their pleasure one or two women from just west of the Pyrenees. I am paying a living wage—so I feel a couple of grand more noble than those ancient lechers. And cleaner—I pay them to penetrate each other—not to be penetrated by me—this way I am above moral or indeed biological rebuke. I barely suffer myself to be touched by them—for their forms, voices, movements are of another universe, and if they touch me this world of music and laughter will dissolve too quickly. I have let the girls change the records at their whim. We have listened to the entirety of *The Stranger*, of *Blind Faith*, and now we are on to *Bitches Brew*—I think I am going to keep these girls on my payroll for the entire future. This journey is only in its first instar. How many costumes will I shed—how many histories will I don—in this my period of transfiguration? On the surface I am old and rugged, but on the inside I take on all forms. I have no way of predicting what tones my voice will produce from moment to moment—how can I predict where my soul will wander?

14

I will never leave Paris. I have found a peculiar path
through her, along which I wander anonymous and
free—the path from assignation to assignation—the
one unaware of the other—the other unaware of the
one—and I have become intimate with the infinitude
of streets where I can disappear and reappear without reason or explanation—just as I used to do in the
wilderness—and for a just a modicum of my time—
which is nothing if not used for the gratification of the
body—for the price of just a pinch of time I can disappear through a trap door in history—there—I am gone—
and yet I recur—and no one is any the wiser—for the
act of disappearance and reappearance is performed
in a vault to which not even I know the code. And if
you crack the code it cracks itself in that instant—and
behind the door there is an impostor murmuring the
preface to my journal all in white letters, so that his
narrative sounds like haze on a mountain. And though

you might be tempted to try that door again, the entire architecture of the vestibule has disappeared, and you cannot recall what it was you were looking for.

I understand now that my love—for you—for everyone—is a satellite—a moon—a vagabond, and not even I understand how or why it chooses its objects. Night to night—even moment to moment—there is no predictable attachment to a theme, to a pattern, to a color, to a texture, to an age, to a language, to a particular vision of you. And my love for each of you is preserved in amber like my memory of the young Carlita at her wood stove in the primeval forests of Bribri—for instead of waiting until my affection melts and is washed away by the rain, I leave and find you in another form. In place of the murdered holograms that used to inhabit my mind, I now see the walls of my museum papered with impressionistic bliss. Two lips barely open, their bearer speechless, her fingers reach for mine under the bar in trails of settled smoke. The night—the final movement.

The affection we hold for those we have never met—our ability to see directly through one another's skin to the molten center—our power of metaphysical recognition—is our most ancient, our most spectacular quality—no wonder it is also the most forbidden, the most taboo. Exercising that faculty to the utmost, I have found a new Alicia. She is half Genovese and half Niçoise. She takes care of her father's buildings in the

Latin Quarter—he was a squatter at just the right time and place in the sixties. She is a jazz singer and a creator of outrageous canvases that she sells for a year's wage on the Rue Dauphine. I own a few, and when I leave her I will burn them. Yesterday we walked from her apartment in Les Invalides through the Tuileries and out the Rue de Castiglione and into the aura of the Palais Garnier—I felt your presence and I could not breathe, my legs went numb and weak—I must have looked like a poached fig—but this Alicia put her arms around me and her breast rumbled and fluttered against mine and my suffering was exorcised from me—I felt I was back in Cacao again—I was beating a trail to the top for the first time—breathless, terrified, but ecstatic with the feeling of a centuries-long bond to a ghostly omnipresence. So my new Alicia—and three weeks from now I will tell her it is too painful to possess her at my age—she so near to her birth and I so near to the gates of St. Peter. Alicia . . . she appreciates the mobiles of Calder—how they symbolize and crucify our reliance on language to express our fantasies—why not images, horizons, hues, gestures, our eyes, our closed eyes? Why, this Alicia tells me, do we not express our dreams in movement, in silence, in temperature? Alicia's lips are the pale of an island sunset, and she keeps them unpainted because that is the one thing I ask of her—to keep herself free of embellishment. She is not your first image of beauty—but she is your first image of sensuality—and when you press your body against her you will understand me.

I was never skilled at existence. Since I can remember, my fascination with small things otherwise ignored made me an outcast—and the fascination itself was so overwhelming that it made simple daily tasks impossible. I remember walking the streets, simply destroyed over the fact that in some measure of days, my stream of consciousness would be polluted by a meeting of the department administration, or by a form that needed to be returned to the telephone company—or by a cheque that needed to be written and signed just so. And once dressed in miserable suit and miserable tie and miserable leather shoes—once headed to the post office or the bank—I would fixate on the way my steps struck a rhythm against the pavement—and otherwise contemplate my mode of suicide. By freight train—by noose—by simple refusal to breathe—by simple refusal to exist—by random disappearance—by pills—by accident—by street crossing while dreaming—by getting lost in drink. Drink always seemed best, because there was a process to it that one could enjoy—something like a bullfighter who never retires—eventually that beast will skewer him—but the intervening years will be full of indulgence in shiny distractions.

We have not yet investigated, as a human race, what happens when one is alone. In my studies of capuchin monkeys, a pariah from a troop is as good as dead—not for lack of protection or for lack of food—but by means of sadness. If you get a glimpse into the eyes of the pariah, there is an aura of being lost to the world—but the monkey seems to know that weeping will do him no good—so he holds on to his glassy tears—they serve to blur the image of his plight—they buffer him against the immutable eternity of his reality. He wanders, he thinks of his mother. He replays that last retort of the alpha male who banished him from the comfort and the beauty and the daily rhythms of companionship. He replays the message inherent in the alpha's dread expression—you are nothing to me—you are nothing to anyone—let your body lapse. Finally he drapes himself over a tree limb, just as he did his mother's back when he was an infant. He feels the pangs of fear inside his chest. He feels the stillness of the tree. And he wishes to be more still, more strong, more timeless. This his final wish actually does reach the skies—the last one seems to be the only one with any buoyancy. Nature listens—she mercifully takes back her own—and with a moan at the darkest hour of night the pariah disappears.

So it goes with men—only I seem to be different. In my solitude, which I encounter more and more now that Alicia the Second has stormed from my life screaming, writhing, pulling at her hair and fine skin—beseeching anyone who will listen to capture and jail and castrate me like a Victorian schizophrenic—in my solitude I am delivered from all loneliness and frustration, and I start tracing the fingernail of my mind down the coast from Tortuguero to Manzanillo—where the rain will never stop—where the rain, when it comes, is composed of tears of joy wrung from the eyes of the gods in their naked two step that keeps on repeating—keeps on repeating—keeps on repeating—keeps on repeating—keeps. . .

. . . on repeating—and the rains come on in an ear-shattering cry of sky against earth—to turn in the new seeds—to send the lantern-bearers of evil back to their caves and tree nooks—to make something grow again.